The Woman's Book of Superlatives

Catherine Lim

TIMES BOOKS INTERNATIONAL
Singapore • Kuala Lumpur

Reprinted 1993, 2000

Published by Times Books International
An imprint of Times Media Private Limited
A member of the Times Publishing Group
Times Centre
1 New Industrial Road
Singapore 536196
Fax: (65) 285 4871 Tel: (65) 284 8844
e-mail: te@corp.tpl.com.sg

Online Bookstore:
http://www.timesone.com.sg/te

Times Subang
Lot 46, Subang Hi-Tech Industrial Park
Batu Tiga
40000 Shah Alam
Selangor Darul Ehsan
Malaysia
Fax & Tel: (603) 736 3517
E-mail: cchong@tpg.com.my

Printed in Singapore

ISBN 981 204 401 9

Contents

Prologue: Images

I listen and hear her voice which she tries to keep steady with resoluteness of purpose but which is dangerously close to a sob.

"You held out your hand for an egg," she says, "and fate put into it a scorpion. Show no consternation: close your fingers firmly upon the gift; let it sting through your palm. Never mind; in time, after your hand and arm have swelled and quivered long with torture, the squeezed scorpion will die, and you will have learned a great lesson: how to endure without a sob."

And it is invariably at this point that I see her tilt her head backwards, a simple action which has the marvellously manifold function of suppressing the sob, setting a final stamp of defiance on her little speech and preventing the secret tears from spilling out of her eyes.

This admonition to women saddens me. It conjures up for me images of suffering women for all time, beginning with, appropriately, that of the female skeleton in a Stone Age settlement with a stake driven through where the heart was, and a little pile of bones between the parted skeleton legs. The archaeologist's surmise was that the woman had been found by her husband to be with child, not his, and in the tribe's ritual of punishment reserved for such faithlessness, he had driven the stake through her and the child out of her in a simultaneous panging of birth and death.

I see also the Victorian woman in long black dress, gaunt after eight childbirths and soon to die from her ninth, and the Chinese peasant woman, sick with anxiety as the mid-wife pulls out of her yet another girl-child, and she knows she has lost the last chance to redeem herself with her husband.

A woman's fears are inseparable from her fecundity; she dies in childbirth, in more than one sense of the word.

And now I see the Indian Suttee Woman, the African Infibulated Woman, the Chinese Bound Feet Woman. Sarojini, hair streaming, in her widow's white sari, leaps into the flames engulfing her husband's corpse as it lies on the pile of wood, and after her, a whole line-up of white-clad widows, freed from this barbarous custom, but burning themselves in perpetual suttee in their extreme poverty and isolation. Onika, the girl-child whose lips are sewn together for a man's pleasurable bursting on the wedding night, and which will be sewn up again, whenever he is absent as assurance of his exclusive rights to her body. My great grandmother who is told to kneel down before the ancestral altars in thanksgiving for the great good luck of being sold as a child concubine into a wealthy family. I see Great Grandmother's little girl body convulse in pain and hear her screams as they bind her feet tighter and still tighter, her mother bending to hold and comfort her: "Hush, little one, you mustn't cry. Think of the time when you will be a very beautiful woman and all the men will be asking for you!" And perhaps she is already thinking of the Old One, very wealthy indeed, whose particular delectation is to see the young white bodies, naked except for their little dolls' feet in silken dolls' shoes, come swaying towards him like flowers on stalks.

The images will not go away. More come crowding into my mind, in a crazy scrambling of time and place, for neither history nor geography has been protective of women.

The slave girl in the cotton plantation carried to the bed of her coarse owner who will then signal for his son to carry her to his; the ten thousand women and girls whose brutalised bodies are anonymously swept under the blanket term of 'The Rape of Nanking' in the history books; the equally nameless Indian women whose dowries are inadequate and so they are burnt by their husbands who then go to report kitchen accidents; the little eleven-year-old girl from Hyderabad whose name Bina is known because on the plane with the sixty-year-old Arab to whom her father has just sold her in marriage, she has dared to sob out her story to the stewardess who alerts the police; my grandmother whose feet were never bound but whose life was; the little Singapore schoolgirl Pei Yin who died from a very messy abortion and whose father went scot-free.

Scorpion-receivers, all, and Charlotte Brontë's advice is for them: endure.

The receiving and enduring could begin very early; in Pei Yin's case, it was about the time she sprouted breasts and became a woman, and in Bina's case, even younger, for she was only eleven and probably had not yet had her first menstruation. Indeed, it could begin before the girl's life could begin, and I am now thinking of the newborn baby girls in China, strangled with bare hands, suffocated in trays of ash, thrown into wells, thrown into rubbish dumps or the mud of rice-fields, because the new population policy allows for only one child, and parents' hopes for a male child are pinned on that one chance.

I want so much to know why this woman who obsesses me has given such fatal advice which has been received down the ages, and retrospectively, right back to the Cave Woman who died with her baby. I want the years between us – one hundred and eighty six, to be exact – to melt away, so that I can meet her face to face and talk to her, this intense, strange, small woman who obsesses me.

Her only existing portrait shows a pixie-like but strong face with small, purposeful mouth and dark brown hair, probably her best feature, neatly parted in the middle and utterly smoothed on each side, in the manner we have come to associate with Victorian spinster ladies (she married but was dead within a year, owing to complications in a pregnancy that her doctor thought could not be sustained by such a tiny body, almost like a child's). There is a small smile playing around her intense mouth, perhaps of triumph at overcoming the scorpion at last.

Over the years, these words of hers have become points of reference by which I try to have a clearer understanding of her thoughts and feelings.

"You held out your hand for an egg and fate put into it a scorpion." By shifting the blame to fate, she had absolved her Christian God of the responsibility for going back on his own promise. She must have asked for good health for

her beloved sisters; she watched them die, one by one, undernourished, lonely, broken. She must have asked for strength for the brother to turn over a new leaf, to stop the drinking, the opium addiction, the irresponsibilities which were draining his sisters of their strength and meagre resources; she watched him die too, a raving lunatic, and by that time her thoughts must already have shaped into the philosophy of that proud claim of endurance of her sex: "This would never have happened with a woman."

But the egg she held out her hand most eagerly for and had a scorpion put into it instead, was the gift of a man's love. She had fallen secretly, passionately in love with a professor, a married man. No, to ask for his love was too much. She asked for mere friendship, expressed in just a few letters that would be enough to sustain her in her desolation. There was one which she had read so many times in the privacy of her room and solitary rambles on those wild windswept moors that she knew every word by heart and every meaning accreted around every word by the heart's yearning. She sent off one letter after another, and waited, but received none. She became desperate, comparing herself, in one of her letters, to the starving beggar who will not dare ask for the food from the table, only wait for the crumbs to fall off it.

Still, no letter came and at last she gave up hope and fell into a dull despair. Unknown to her, her letters had been torn up and dropped into the wastebasket by the professor and later secretly retrieved by the professor's wife, a most formidable woman who meticulously put the pieces together.

"Close your fingers firmly upon the gift; let it sting through your palm." The gift of a man's rejection can be too great for a woman to bear, and then fantasy, as only a lonely woman can weave, must come to the rescue. In one of her novels, Charlotte Brontë describes how a young woman secretly falls in love with a professor (who is not married) teaching in the same school as herself. The secretive, jealous headmistress of the school watches her movements closely. One cold, bleak afternoon, as she sits alone at her desk, she falls asleep and in the gathering gloom wakes up to find that somebody had tenderly placed a warm shawl round her shoulders as she slept: she has no doubt who that somebody is, and that her love for him and his for her will grow and overcome all obstacles in a touching fulfilment at the end.

Now I am certain nothing of the sort happened in her real life: the professor never approached her as she was sleeping, with that thoughtful, comforting shawl. She made it all up, to distract herself from the sting of the scorpion through her fingers.

There must have been a time of secret raging against the cruel gap between dream and reality, before the calm clarity of that advice, for Charlotte Brontë once described herself as a "hearty hater." I copied the words down when I first came upon them and then tested them upon the tongue, struck by the powerful mutual reinforcement of sound and sense. If you pronounce the words slowly, deliberately, you too will be struck by the effect of the repeated "h" and "t" sounds: they swell the already charged meaning of a hate that needs to be continually fed, like an appetite insatiable of food or sex.

And then the anger must have subsided into resignation at last, not the confused, contemptible kind but the proud acceptance of destiny – "the great lesson: how to endure without a sob."

'Never mind.' But the body minds, surely, when it is stung, bitten, poked, battered, invaded, infibulated, bound, burnt, burst. If it were not smaller and weaker, or continually convulsed and drained by childbearing and childfeeding, it could have fought back. But as it is, women have to endure by biological fiat.

"Never mind." It is not the body only. The mind minds, too, and women grow mad from their fears and longings, for women's mind is one fibre with her sensitive, convulsive, procreative, nurturative body. Perhaps the mind minds more than the body.

I see them now and hear them, hardly images, rather fragments as from recollected dreams, and faint cries, like the ancestral voices calling from afar. The woman standing by a storm-lashed coast waiting on a promise that will never be kept; the woman ghost seen with her baby near the pond where she drowned twenty years ago; the four Korean sisters who took poison together because, as they said in their note, they were sad that the expense of their upkeep was depriving their only brother of a higher education; the battered Singapore housewife who went back again and again to her husband because he sobbed on her shoulder and told her he couldn't live without her.

When a friend of mine was frantic to get back her husband who had gone to live with a younger woman, her family took her to consult a fortune teller who advised her to do nothing rash but wait, for he would come back. She waited for eight years and true enough, he came back, and they said, "See, we told you." When my marriage was about to break up, my relatives and friends counselled patience and waiting: it seems a woman waits all her life, she waits to get married, she waits for her first-born, she waits for the children to grow up, she waits for a husband or lover to come back.

I walk into a bookshop and I see, in the section called "Inspirational", books by women for women, with heart-breaking titles – "Women who love too much", "Women who can't forget", "Women who can't say no".

"But men are scorpion-receivers too." This from a male friend when I told him of the stories I wanted to write. He being very dear, I did not want to quarrel, so I merely said, "Yes, but men are never told to endure. It would be unthinkable for men to endure."

"You know," he said, not wishing to be put off, "that there are other ways in which you women receive the scorpions. Are you going to write about these too?"

"I know," I said, "and yes, I'm going to write about those too. We can fling the scorpion back at the giver. Or de-fang it and be comfortable with it. We can secretly fatten it and return it as a gift. We can domesticate it and make it serve us. But mainly we endure, with or without a sob. We don't have much choice." Life and literature are full of the superlatives of woman's endurance, also of her revenge.

"I don't like you very much when you talk like that, and I don't want to read your stories, they sound horrible," he said. And was not the less dear for saying that.

"That's the trouble," I sighed. "The stories you

perpetuate of us are so unreal. You sing paeans to us; you put us on pedestals, in the shining clouds of myths and legends as your goddesses, warrior queens, glorious martyrs, virgin brides. They have nothing to do with the reality. Perhaps they are to compensate for the reality." We were silent for a while, not wanting to risk a quarrel, the secret time of our being together being so rare and therefore so happy.

"Are you going to write about women who receive the eggs?" he asked suddenly. "I should think you would want to write about the egg-receivers, too."

"Yes," I said, "but not yet. Not yet."

I

The Enemy

O Woman! How should we even begin to extol your beauty that has kept us in thrall through the ages? I, Love's humblest acolyte who have pledged myself to your service am, alas, wordless in the commencement of that service. But I shall not be daunted. I shall begin with the beauty of your breasts. And I shall make bold to borrow the words of the Creator Himself, for was it not He who inspired this loveliest of descriptions of a woman's body, to culminate in the breasts themselves? 'How beautiful are thy feet with shoes. O prince's daughter! The joints of thy thighs are like jewels, the work of the hands of a cunning workman. Thy navel is like a round goblet, which wanteth not liquor; thy belly is like a heap of wheat set about with lilies. Thy two breasts are like roes that are twins. This thy stature is like to a palm tree, and thy breasts to clusters of grapes.'

O Woman!
O Woman nonpareil!

(From The Woman's Book Of Superlatives)

The girl hated her breasts because they were the cause of all her troubles. Confronting her now in the bright afternoon light in her bedroom, they shocked by their newness and rawness: two hard cones, pink-tipped, suddenly grown out of the flatness, and warning of a rampage of further growth by the little eager shooting pains inside them. She picked up a towel hurriedly and draped it over the mirror, blocking them out.

The sweetness of her days was gone, stolen by the breasts. In the classroom she sat hunched, her chest drawn in, her shoulders pushed out to force a retreat of the enemy, and in the playground, it was the same, whether she was skipping or running. She watched for their bouncing and was relieved to find that as yet that was not happening, no matter how vigorously she skipped or hopped. Would they soon grow into a size and softness when the bouncing would begin and the skipping and laughter end?

The thought filled her with dread. Oh, the innocence of flatness! Her flat friends, when they got hot and sweaty in the playing field, pulled up their blouses to wipe their faces. She could not do that now.

They were defiant breasts, constantly defying the concavity of the hunched chest. She had an idea to defeat them. First, she slipped over her head a small singlet and unrolled it down over them, flattening them out. Next she slipped on one more such singlet and a sleeveless T-shirt that effectively erased them and finally, she put on her white cotton school blouse, carefully buttoning it all the way up front. She looked at herself in the mirror and was satisfied. Defeated at last.

Thus barricaded, the enemy gave no more trouble. But the weather did. In the blistering heat of the cement-box classroom of forty pupils and one weakly rotating fan, the sweat trickled down her face and neck and gathered in a hot pool at her breasts. She went on resolutely doing her work at her desk, a calm centre in a frenzied sea of fluttering paper fans and blowing cheeks. Her wet hair clung to her face and neck in sorry tendrils but she went on quietly working, aware that Mrs Tan's eyes had come to rest on her and were studying her closely.

"Pei Yin, I would like you to see me in the Counselling Room after school today."

In the Counselling Room, Mrs Tan made her take off each sodden layer, until the breasts, newly released, burst into view once more, and she hung her head in shame.

"You could have been over-heated, bundled up like that in this weather, and got a seizure. Tell your mother to get you a proper bra. Young growing girls like you must know how to take care of their bodies. And don't hunch again. I've been noticing."

The breasts, now snugly fitted and cupped, poked triumphantly through the thin cotton cloth of her school-blouse, and she took to carrying around a large paper file which she held, clasped to her chest.

And then, through a happy discovery, there was no more need for the file and the embarrassment. She discovered that three other girls in her class had sprouted breasts and were wearing bras. To ascertain the fact, she had pretended to pat each of them on the back and then had surreptitiously felt for the bra strap: she was not alone! Shared misery was that much less misery; within months, breasts spread as in an epidemic and by the time the last girl to have them had them and came to class wearing a bra, Pei Yin's misery had vanished completely.

Mrs Tan singled her out from among all the rest for warm praise: "You look very healthy and pretty now, Pei Yin and how is the project coming along? I see you are working very hard at it."

A rare radiance broke upon the girl's face. Yes, she told her teacher, the project for the School's Family Joy Competition, was coming along very nicely, and she had got some new pictures to paste in the book and found a suitable poem to write under one of the pictures.

No, the trouble of her breasts did not come from school; if not for the little pricks of pain shooting all over, even in the armpits, she could almost forget their existence entirely.

Sitting in the bus, she was aware of a massive thigh pushed against her own. Staring straight ahead, she moved away a little, and the thigh followed. She continued staring straight ahead. A newspaper went rustling up and then fingers under cover of the newspaper, forced themselves under her thigh and began attacking her there. She held her breath. Somebody buzzed for the next stop, and when the bus lurched to a standstill, she picked up her schoolbag, stood up and tried to get around the massive legs determinedly planted to obstruct her way and jiggling up and down with menacing nonchalance.

"Excuse me," she said in a small voice. One of the legs moved, and again, under cover of the newspaper, the hand shot out a second time and touched her on the left breast, accompanied by a low brutal gurgle. She ran down the steps in the bus and found herself at an unfamiliar bus-stop, but no matter, she could easily find her way home. The pain of the touch was still there. She was not allowed to spit in a public place, but she would remember to do it when she reached home, spitting being, as she had observed in her mother and the women neighbours, a symbolic discharge of the enemy's poison that would surely rebound on him. She hated the men in the buses who had pinched, touched, stroked or rubbed themselves against her ever since the breasts came, but no, the real trouble did not come from them, for it was in her power to remove herself from them.

Weather and breasts again conspired. This time it was not the heat, but pouring rain. She came home from school, totally drenched. The rain reduced her thin white T-shirt and cotton bra to transparent cellophane against which her breasts now pressed forth in the full flagrancy of their size, shape and colour: she might as well be naked. She stood near the door, pinned to the wall by the intensity of her father's gaze upon those breasts, as he came out of his room to meet her. His eyes roamed the exposed concentric circles of beauty, inwards from the smooth white roundness to the small light brown patches to the innermost pink tips, and then outwards, till the beauty was fully savoured.

She felt a sickness deep inside her stomach.

"Ai-yah, little Pei Pei! you are all wet! So you were caught in the rain? Why didn't you take an umbrella to school with you this morning? Now you are sure to catch cold, little Pei Pei, ai-yah – " The stream of niceties was a prelude only, to be got out of the way quickly, as he advanced upon her still standing helplessly against the wall, and the breasts – oh hateful things! – perfectly moulded to the transparent wetness of her clothes, continued to beckon and invite.

"Ah –," said the father in final advance, then stopped, turning round at the sound of a door being flung open and footsteps approaching. It was the other daughter and he said, affably, "See, Mee Yin, your little sister's all wet. She should get a towel to dry herself quickly – "

Ignoring him, Mee Yin who called herself Debbie and sometimes Desiree, said sternly to her younger sister, "Go and dry yourself immediately. You may borrow my hair dryer. And next time don't come into the house with your breasts all exposed like that. There are people around who are only waiting for this to happen!" She flung a contemptuous sidelong glance at the father who was still smiling, but a little sheepishly, as he rubbed the back of his neck and continued to say, "Ai-yah, you'll catch cold!"

Debbie/Desiree's breasts were no enemy. She cultivated them for good purpose. At McDonald's, where she worked, she wore a bra specially constructed to push breasts, no matter how floppy, into a startling twinning of perfect roundness. The waitress' uniform of puff-sleeved, high-collared blouse did not allow for this round ripeness to present itself, but an undoing of the first three buttons down the front ensured a tantalising peek or two, especially when she bent over the tables with her tray of hamburgers and coke.

She saw a hand shoot out towards her and was not in time to arrest its advance; in an instant, deft fingers had wedged something into the tight cleavage. She laid the tray carefully on the table before standing up to put her hand into her blouse, pull out a crumpled note and return it to its owner who was watching her, grinning. "For you, honey, you keep it," he said with a wink and left. It was a fifty dollar note. She put it in the pocket of her apron.

She let her boy friend Salleh who worked in the same place, touch her breasts sometimes; often she pouted, scolded, screamed and pushed his hand away, aware that these, her greatest asset, were not for foolish squandering.

Their beauty was strangely enhanced by the streaks of brown liquid that had splashed on them. This the father had not expected when he had knocked his mug of coffee against her as they passed each other in the kitchen, and he was able to take in the strangely compelling view of a delicately branching pattern of dark brown ribbons on perfect whiteness of breasts before snapping out of the awe to grab a kitchen towel, apologise profusely, and attempt to wipe off the stains.

"You don't dare touch me!" screamed Debbie/Desiree, pushing him away with such violence that he fell backwards and lay slumped against the legs of a table. "You did that on purpose, you dirty old man! I saw you do it on purpose. Wait till I tell my boyfriend about you. He'll beat you up! Now you've dirtied my dress, and I'm late for work! You're a dirty old man! I'll get my boyfriend to bash you up!" And that was the last time he had tried to touch her.

Pei Yin felt safe with Older Sister. She shared the other bedroom in the flat with her, and even if they forgot to lock the door at night, she was not afraid. Lock the bedroom door, lock the bathroom door. The bathroom door had a hole made by the rotting wood. She had stuffed that with a piece of rag; it had been poked off, and she had stuffed another, this time more tightly.

"You listen carefully to me, Pei Yin," said Older Sister with authority, although she was only three years older.

"Yes, Older Sister," said Pei Yin.

"You are a big girl now and you've got to be more careful. Don't be in the house alone with *him*." Pei Yin noticed that Older Sister never referred to the father as 'Father.' "We bear his name but he's not our real father," she sneered, "Stay in school as long as you can, and don't come home before Mother or I do. Mother says she can't come home before four. Why don't you stay in school till then and wait in the void deck downstairs where you can do your work while waiting for her to come back?"

The Family Joy Project which Pei Yin was now very much occupied with, would allow her to stay in the school library till well past five if she wished.

"All right, but make sure you are never alone in the house with him. Why were you watching TV with him on the same sofa last night? I saw him sitting very close to you."

Pei Yin explained tearfully that as part of the Family Joy Project, the girls had to watch the Cosby Show and comment in class on the happy family relationships they had observed. She did not tell Older Sister that at one point, as she was writing down an observation on a piece of paper on her lap, the father's hand had suddenly reached up inside her blouse and touched the curved underside of her left breast; she sat totally still for a few seconds, staring ahead, while the fingers played and the pyjama-clad body shifted, moved closer and thrust itself outwards upon the couch. Then she jumped up and went into her room, and the father continued to watch TV, his arms now across his chest and his hands tucked in his armpits. She did not forget to spit when she later went into the bathroom.

"You are a big girl now, Pei Yin," said her mother who the month before had brought home a box of sanitary towels for her. Mrs Tan, Older Sister, Mother, they looked at her breasts, called her 'big girl' and took away the sweetness of the small girl years. She hated being a 'big girl'.

"You must know what to do now," said her mother sorrowfully, the sorrow intensified by the prospect of interminable years of backbreaking work at the small food stall she ran at a school. Widowed with two small daughters, she had married a man who promised to expand the food stall into a thriving canteen business but who, over the years, had claimed a succession of small ailments and ended up idling at home.

"Poor little daughter," said the mother tearfully, stroking her face. "You are so innocent and ignorant, not like Older Sister who is so clever and knows how to take care of herself. Do take care, Little One. Your mother has been a great fool, but what is there to do now? Your mother does not want anything bad to happen to you. It is good that you are staying back in school in the afternoons. You are doing something that makes you very happy, Little Daughter? I see it is a big book with plenty of beautiful pictures and much writing." And she took her daughter's face in her hands and smiled proudly.

The pictures were spread around her on the floor, ready to be sorted out and pasted in the big book with the creamy pristine pages. Some old Christmas and New Year cards lay nearby, held down by a pair of scissors, the remains of a large collection that by the transforming power of scissors, paste and crayons, became dazzling daisies, roses, stars, moons, bells, fruit, bows, rainbows, Chinese dragons, puppy heads, kitten heads and perfectly shaped human hearts to be commandeered for whatever decorative purpose their creator intended. The best of the cards had been put aside for the supreme honour of servicing the book's title: letters laboriously traced upon them, carefully cut out and then put together proclaimed "FAMILY JOY by TEO PEI YIN" in uncompromising columns and blocks of purple, red, blue, pink and gold.

Across the heaven of a pastel blue page flew Tinker Bell and Peter Pan hand in hand, shedding a million tiny silver stars, ingeniously fashioned out of discarded chocolate wrapping. Blue page, yellow page, mauve page: the colours provided matching backgrounds, thus blue pages were skies and sparkling water, yellow were golden chicks, buttercups and blond children, mauve were Victorian ladies in soft dresses and parasols and hyacinths in bowls. She enclosed the pictures with whirls and whorls of colour, selecting carefully from a range of twenty-four pens in a box that a classmate had agreed to lend her for the day.

But these, despite the opulence, were preliminaries only, to lead to the true theme of the book, the joy of the family, for evidence of which Pei Yin had amassed a roomful of glossy magazines, advertisements, posters, tourist brochures, calendars, postcards, greeting cards. The Prince and Princess of Wales with their two sons in the garden of their country home, the Cosby family in a laughing entanglement of arms and legs, a sunny family on the beach with their dog wearing a red cap, cut out from a Qantas Airlines poster – the happy families repeated themselves down the pages, culminating in a picture of the Holy Family, St Joseph and the Virgin Mary with their hands prayerfully clasped while they looked upon the Baby Jesus in the hay, radiating light. Beneath this picture, Pei Yin had copied, in flawless script, God's own impassioned rhetoric: "If you ask your father for a loaf of bread, will he give you a stone? If you ask him for an egg, will he give you a scorpion?" It was Mrs Tan's favourite quotation.

The scorpion's poison as yet lay outside the pale of the happy family pictures; it would have been incongruous cast in the midst of so much brightness and hope. For Pei Yin's happy talk and laughter these days as she cut and pasted, drew and wrote, re-drew and re-wrote, were based on the hope of securing the glittering prize of prizes in the school competition – a silver trophy, with the name of the winner engraved. Hope sang, hope whistled a happy tune which subsided into anxious silence as a shadow, long and purposeful, fell across the page bordered by red Chinese dragons. Pei Yin did not look up; she continued the pasting, while the shadow moved and shifted and finally settled in a dense patch on top of her.

"Ai-yah, what beautiful pictures you have, Little Pei

Pei!" said the father, bending over and smiling broadly. "And what beautiful handwriting! You are a very clever girl, Pei Pei."

What happened? she thought. He was supposed to be at a relative's house that evening; that was what he had told Mother. The persistent warning from Mother and Older Sister not to be alone in the flat with the father now shaped into fearsome reality: they were alone, and neither Mother nor Older Sister would be back for some time.

"What are you doing, Little Pei Pei? Tell Father what you are doing." He squatted down beside her, his arms hanging amiably between his legs, his face close to hers, but his hands were as yet untouching. She shrank into herself.

"Why are you afraid of your father, Little Daughter?"

She had frozen into immobility, a pink and blue bird limp in one hand, the scissors in the other. He stood up and she broke out of the immobility to put both bird and scissors on the floor, get up quickly and run into her room. Bolting the door, she sat on her bed, panting. She began to cry.

She heard him moving about, then saw his shadow from under her locked door.

"Little Daughter, I've brought you a present, would you like to have a look at it?"

Never receive gifts from strangers, both Mother and Older Sister had warned. Never receive gifts from fathers.

The shadow lingered, then moved away. She lay still on her bed, worrying about her uncompleted Family Joy Project scattered on the floor. The metal gate clanged. Mother was home! Pei Yin got up quickly to rescue her project. Outside her door stood a box of magic colouring pens – and there were thirty-six of them. Pei Yin gasped. She had never seen such a magnificent array of colours. Reject the gift. Never receive a gift from the enemy. Pei Yin stepped over the box and let it lie there. The next morning, when she woke up and opened the door to have a look, it was gone.

Mrs Tan allowed extra time for the completion of the project. The silver trophy stood in a glass case on the wall in the school assembly area and inspired last-minute feverish activity. The generous classmate who had lent the box of magic pens was generous no longer in the new momentum of rivalry. Pei Yin fretted over her inability to put the finishing touches to the last few pages; she pleaded and the classmate who had stolen a peep at Pei Yin's work and then recoiled in horror at the meagreness of her own, snatched up the precious box of pens, removed herself to another corner of the classroom and tried frantically to make up for lost time.

I must win the trophy, thought Pei Yin, looking around for a similar box to borrow. Mrs Tan, at the door, called to her. She turned round and went pale with fear, for the father was standing there too, a crumpled shirt over his singlet and not even properly buttoned, and an old pair of khaki trousers over his pyjama trousers. In his hands he held, shyly, the box of thirty-six magic pens.

"Say thank you to your father, Pei Yin," said Mrs Tan sharply. "He's come all the way to bring you these lovely pens for your project. Where are your manners?" She felt sorry for the man, shy, poor, uneducated.

Pei Yin said 'Thank you' tremblingly and received the

gift. She would not tell Older Sister about this. Mrs Tan later said, as she observed her using the pens to complete the project, "I'm rather surprised and disappointed in you, Pei Yin. I thought you knew better than to treat your father in that way. He must have spent a lot of money on those pens. And then to take the trouble to come all the way." The man would have come by bus or bicycle; such as he could not afford a car, such as he spoke no English, had bad teeth and deferred to daughters who were ashamed of him.

And then Mrs Tan had an idea. Its relevance, indeed necessity, for any meaning at all for the programme that she had initiated in the school in her capacity as Counsellor, was so obvious she was ashamed it had never occurred to her before. She announced to the girls that she would give them one more day for the submission of their various projects for the Family Joy Competition; they cheered.

"There's something else I want you to do," she said, and the cheers subsided into attentiveness. "I want you, in the true spirit of this competition, to dedicate your project to your daddy." No cheers, but some faces lit up with daughterly affection, and continued to be attentive for more instructions.

"I want you," said Mrs Tan in the confident glow of a job about to be very well done, "to take your book home to your daddy this evening, tell him what it is about and say you have done it for him. As proof that you have actually done what I told you, because some of you are naughty girls who don't follow all instructions," here the girls giggled, rather liking that description of themselves, "you are required to get your daddy's signature on the last page of your book, and also whatever he may wish to write. It does not matter if it is not in the English language," she added.

Someone asked, "Can I ask my mummy to sign too?" and Mrs Tan said, "Yes, if you like. But it's Daddy's signature that I want. And I want all of you to tell one another in class what your daddy said and did. We'll have a nice sharing session."

Pei Yin hung around nervously and anxiously, waiting for her mother to leave for work; Older Sister had left much earlier.

"Aren't you going to school?" said her mother. A classmate was coming, she said, to meet her in a short while and they would go to school together; she needed help to carry some things borrowed from Teacher for her project. Her mother took much longer to finish her coffee; Pei Yin fidgeted, ready in her school uniform, her school bag bulging with things, her Family Joy book in a separate large paper bag.

Alone in the flat with the father at last, her heart thumping so wildly she thought she was going to fall down and be very sick, she took the book out of the paper bag and slowly walked to the father's room, stopping by the door. He was in bed, reading a Chinese newspaper, and at the sight of her, he sat up and pulled off his glasses.

The spasm of surprise over, he said, "Eh, Little Daughter? You want something?" Biting the ends of his spectacles, he studied her with the rare pleasure of an unobstructed view: no hunched shoulders, no turning away. She continued standing at the door, wanting to speak to him, not finding speech. A situation of unspeakable promise, he realised, had presented itself to him, and for a moment he was struck dumb by the sheer wonder of it all. But he soon scrambled out of bed, knocking down spectacles and newspaper and went to her at the door.

"Little Pei Pei, you want something. What can your father do for you?"

She pushed towards him the book, beautifully bound and redolent of roses and hearts, and asked for his signature.

"Ah, you want me to sign this beautiful book?" he said, and the book took on the fresh aspect of an accomplice.

"Come, come, put it on the table here and I'll find a pen," and he led her into the room. "Where's my pen? Where are my glasses? I must put on my glasses so that I can write my name properly in my daughter's beautiful book!"

It will all be over and done with soon, thought Pei Yin with desperation. The harder part was to come. It was a necessary condition for the competition, Teacher said, and they were to talk about it during the sharing session in class.

Pei Yin with new resolution moved up to the father and put her arms around him. A kiss too, said Teacher. That would make Daddy so proud and happy.

"Ah!" he said, dizzy with the wondrousness of the turn of events, and determined no wondrousness should distract flesh from its long-awaited purpose.

He said, hoarse with urgency, "I'll sign afterwards," and lifted her to bring to his bed.

* * *

"Pei Yin, whatever's the matter with you?" cried the startled Mrs Tan for there stood before her a ghost, wild-eyed and white, the blood drained completely from her face, her mouth opening and closing in little animal noises. "Pei Yin, what's the matter? Are you ill? Is it the project –" And it was precisely at this moment that the girl realised she had forgotten to bring the book; her precious book was at that moment lying on the father's bed.

"My project," she gasped and began to look around wildly.

"My project, I forgot to bring it!" She began to scream hysterically, from a further onslaught of that darkness that had enveloped her as she stumbled out of the room, running blindly into a wall before she found the open door, and again as she rushed into the bathroom and struggled through the raw pitilessness of sweat and blood and slime. Choking, she had tried to spit out the poison, but the scorpion had bitten too deep for that.

She threw herself upon the floor, crying dismally, and Mrs Tan caught hold of her and with the help of another teacher, carried her to the school lounge where they put her in a large comfortable chair and tried to soothe her. She continued crying, in great sobs that wracked her little body, while Mrs Tan held her, stroked her hair and patted her gently till the sobbing subsided.

"Don't worry about the project," she said soothingly, "You can bring it tomorrow, I don't mind at all. Don't worry," and wondered about the larger agonies, beyond any school project, that this poor, sensitive, overwrought child was privately suffering. She was convinced they had to do with the father, and she wondered, for the hundredth time, about an education system that distanced articulate English-educated daughters from their fumbling illiterate fathers. If guilt was part of this strange child's hysteria, it was no bad thing.

"I have to get my book, or it will be ruined! Please let me go home to get my book!"

The child was becoming hysterical again, and had to be soothed afresh. Somebody brought a hot drink. Mrs Tan, putting her arms tenderly round the poor girl, drew her attention to the clouds that could be seen through the window, amassing with dark power. "See how dark the sky is. See those black clouds. It's going to rain. So you can't go home, or you will get wet and catch cold. It doesn't matter if you can't hand up the project today. It doesn't matter at all. It will make no difference to the competition whatsoever, see? I know how hard you've worked at it. Now take this drink and you'll feel much better."

The rain came down in torrents. Pei Yin watched it with dull, resigned eyes, and Mrs Tan went on talking to her in a soothing voice.

"Try to get some sleep, dear," she said. "Everything will be alright, so you mustn't worry. Okay, Pei Yin?" The rain continued to fall in thick ruthless sheets. Mrs Tan, leaving Pei Yin's side for the first time that strange afternoon in answer to a call, stared in amazement at the visitor standing at the entrance of the school office in a puddle of rain water. He had apparently come in the rain in a hurry, for he had on only a singlet and pyjama trousers, now totally wet and clinging to his undernourished legs. To Mrs Tan's first astonished question about how he had got there in the rain, he shyly pointed to an old bicycle leaning against a dripping tree near the school gate, and to the second question about why he was there, he pulled out of a paper bag the book, but no longer recognisable, for the rainwater had scrambled all the colours into a streaky, brownish mess. A sodden page fell out and the father, laughing nervously, bent to pick up the Holy Family and put it back into the book.

"My daughter forgot to take this to school, so I've brought it," he said simply, and then was gone back into the rain.

Mrs Tan stood for a while, holding the soggy mess, and her eyes filled with tears as she watched the father, a tiny figure now, pedal away in the rain.

"Pei Yin," she said as she returned to where the girl was sitting quietly in the chair, "I've got such good news for you." The girl, suddenly noticing the book, frowned, started up, rushed forward to grab it and gazing upon the desolate remains, sat upon the floor once more and sobbed in the infinitude of woman's sorrow.

"It's okay, it's okay," said Mrs Tan, awed by the power of what she had just witnessed. She picked up the girl and held her close. "We'll not worry about the competition any more, shall we? Anyway, it isn't that important, is it? We'll just forget about it." The good news was not just for the girl alone; it was for all daughters and fathers, and she, in the work to which she had committed herself, would be its humble bearer.

II

For The Gift Of A Man's Understanding

Let me tell you the story of Inanna, the great goddess of the ancient Sumerians. So beloved was she because of her power and wisdom that every year, her High Priestesses received, in her name, streams of devoted men bringing gifts of wheat and fruit, fish and animals, to lay at the goddess's feet. Every year too, there was the Ritual of the Sacred Mating, that is, a High Priestess put to the test young men aspiring to be appointed the year's Shepherd or Damuzi, True Consort of Inanna. And this was how the ritual went: her body, freshly bathed and perfumed and wrapped with her breechcloth and robes, her eyes glowing with kohl, the High Priestess invited the aspirant to prove himself on her bed, to test his fitness as the sacred consort. He, trembling with anxiety, would be led by her to the bed, and she would remind him, even as they were about to climb on to the silken pillows, that even though his gifts of fruit and honey, herbs and plants, flesh and fowl were the best of all, and even though his youthful beauty was unparalleled, he had still not passed the ultimate test:

Only when he has shown his love
When he has pleasured my loins
And I his, on my bed,
Will I show him kindness

And appoint him Damuzi
The Chosen of Inanna's Lap.

(From ***TWBOS****)*

"Good morning, Mr Ong. There's something I would like to talk to you about, if I may. It's very important."

"Sure, Mrs Lee. Do sit down."

"Mr Ong, I hope you don't mind, but I'm going to be extremely frank."

"No, I don't mind at all. Please go on."

"I've been thinking about the matter for a long while, Mr Ong, and in fact have been quite unhappy about it, wondering what I should do. I thought it best to discuss it with you, rather than with my husband."

"You've made me very curious, Mrs Lee. Just what is this matter that's making you so unhappy? And so very nervous. Your hands are trembling. Can I get you a hot drink or something?"

"Oh, no, thank you, Mr Ong, that's very kind of you. You see, Mr Ong, you see, I ... I ..."

"Yes, Mrs Lee? Don't be afraid. Do tell me what's troubling you."

"Mr Ong, I've been working for you now for six months, and I want to say what a very good and generous boss you've been –"

"Surely that's not what's troubling you, Mrs Lee? Do get to the point. We haven't got all morning, you know. There's the Meyer letter we must do this morning."

"Yes, of course, Mr Ong. Oh Mr Ong, please forgive me if I sound too ... too unreasonable but I wish you'd stop touching me ... you know ... touching me ..."

"Oh!"

"Mr Ong, I don't mean to sound rude or accusing, but I get very uncomfortable when you touch me on the ... on the behind and ... and ... in front –"

"I'm sorry, Mrs Lee. I had no idea I was making you so unhappy. I offer no excuses for my behaviour. I assure you it will not happen again. Will that be alright?"

"Yes, Mr Ong. Thank you so much for your understanding."

"Mrs Lee, I can't tell you how truly sorry I am. I deserve all the contempt you can show me, and it will serve me right if you now speak your mind and tell me to my face what you have been suffering all these months because of me."

"Oh, Mr Ong, it will do me good to tell everything, since it has been a wretched secret burdening me. I had nobody to tell it to, knowing nobody would believe me."

"But I do believe you, Mrs Lee, and I believe you must have suffered intensely. So now tell me. There is no greater punishment for a sinful man like me than to have his sins flung in his face."

"Last month, Mr Ong, you called me into your office to handle a fax from Germany. While I was sitting at your table, you suddenly got up, came up to me and sat on the edge of the table, facing me, your fly unzipped. I did not know where to look, and kept my eyes down, but I knew you were looking at me all the time, enjoying my discomfiture."

"I'm really sorry, Mrs Lee. I'm indeed most ashamed –"

"On another occasion, Mr Ong, I was standing beside you with some letters when you suddenly remarked on the pearl necklace I was wearing, got up and pretended to examine it, all the time letting your hand slip lower down my blouse. Fortunately, someone knocked on the door then."

"Mrs Lee, I'm thoroughly ashamed –"

"Then just last week, Mr Ong, you called me into the office and told me you had something interesting to show me and you pulled out of your drawer a magazine opened to show a most disgusting picture of a copulating couple. You asked me, did you not, whether my husband and I had ever tried that position –"

"Mrs Lee, I beg you to stop. I'm most ashamed. I can hardly believe I subjected you to all these indignities –"

"Mr Ong, the very next day after that disgusting picture, you again called me into your office. You were not at your table and as I was looking around, wondering where you were, you called again and this time I saw that you were in the toilet and you said, in a voice that will haunt my worst nightmares, 'Come here, there's something I would like to show you! Quick, it's waiting for you!'"

"Mrs Lee, please forgive me. I'm ready to do anything by way of reparation. Please forgive me."

"Promise me you will never ever do any of those things again, or tell dirty jokes or touch any part of me."

"I promise."

"Promise me you will never do that to any other woman."

"I promise."

"That is all I ask of you, Mr Ong. Thank you."

Helen Lee's fantasies, as she sat half dozing in the bus on the way to work, never shaped around roses and moonlit tenderness, only around a man's understanding of a woman's pain and a sincere promise to stop causing the pain.

Today, she was going to try to make her fantasies come true.

She knocked on the boss's door, her heart pounding wildly.

"Ah, Helen! Here you are! You are a little late, but never mind. Come in, come in."

"Good morning, Mr Ong. There's something I would like to talk to you about, if I may. It's very important."

The tone during the rehearsals was firm; now her voice went all unsteady and her hands began to feel cold. But the opening words had come off right, thank goodness. He looked up and grinned.

"Sure, Helen. Do sit down."

"Mr Ong, I hope you don't mind, but I'm going to be extremely frank."

He continued grinning at her.

"Hey, this is a new you. I've never heard you speak like this before. But of course I don't mind. In fact, I rather like you in this new mood. Shoot!"

"I've been thinking about the matter for a long while, Mr Ong, and in fact have been quite unhappy about it, wondering what I should do. I thought it best to discuss it with you, rather than with my husband."

"Ah, so I take precedence over your husband? That sounds very promising, Helen!" And he gave her a wink.

"Mr Ong, I want to talk about – I would like –"

"What would you like? Goodness, Helen, your hands are trembling! You must be very cold. Come, let me rub them. I'm very good at rubbing."

"Oh, no! No thank you, Mr Ong. Mr Ong, I ... I hope you will understand ... I've been here six months and I enjoy working for you very much –"

"Well, my dear, I'm glad to hear that! So you enjoy working for me? Well, I enjoy working with you too, dear, and perhaps one of these days, it will not be just *with* you, but *on* you and *in* you, I hope. What do you say to that? I love the versatility of the English preposition 'in', don't you? Have you heard the joke about the couple in their cabin on a ship bound for India –"

"Mr Ong, please forgive me if I sound too ... too unreasonable, but I wish you would stop touching me ... you know ... touching me –"

"Ha! Ha! Ha! So that was it. Ha! Ha! Ha! How funny you are. But of course it's unreasonable of you, Helen, to ask me to stop touching you. Very unreasonable indeed. A beautiful woman like you simply cries out to be touched. Look at yourself. Do you look at yourself in the mirror every morning, Helen? And I don't mean with all those clothes on. I suggest you do. Only women with gorgeous bodies like yours have a right to. Excellent way of building self-esteem. But tell me, my dear, when did I last touch you? Where? How? Show me, my dear."

"Mr Ong, you mustn't make fun of me. I'm very serious. I'm very unhappy."

"Tch, tch, tch! I don't want you to be unhappy. You know that's the last thing I want for my efficient, hardworking, totally loyal little secretary. But my dear, you still have not given proof for your accusation. You accused me of touching you. When was that? What did I do?"

"Mr Ong, I was wearing a pearl necklace and you touched it and admired it, but you were only interested in ... in ..."

"In what, my dear? Tell me."

"In touching my breasts, Mr Ong!"

"Ah, how strange the word sounds coming from you. But I like it. You know Helen, I've never heard you say 'breasts' or 'thighs' or 'penis' or 'screw.' It's okay to say them, you know. This is the age of emancipation for women. You say and do exactly what you like. So I touched your breasts, Helen. How did I do it? Like this?"

"Please, Mr Ong. Don't do this to me. This is no time for joking or playing. I'm very unhappy."

"But surely it does no harm to admire a woman's lovely breasts? And you have the loveliest breasts I've ever seen, Helen. Nicer than my wife's. I tell her to use those bras that improve the shape and thrust. What size –"

"Oh, please stop, Mr Ong. I'm only a simple secretary and I have to work hard to support my child who is in hospital and my husband who is at present unemployed –"

"But happily employed in other ways, my dear. How I envy him! While I go home quite tired out and unable to perform my husbandly duties as well as I would like to, he is all fresh and ready for you. How many times –"

"Oh, please stop, Mr Ong!"

"Look at this picture, my dear. Isn't it wonderful that

they can do it in this position? I couldn't if I tried. Maybe I should try –"

"Stop, Mr Ong, please stop!"

He was once more sitting in front of her, his fly unzipped. She ran out, sobbing.

At her desk, she quickly dabbed powder around her eyes, applied fresh lipstick and prepared for the day's work. Appealing to a man's compassion for a woman did not work. Indeed a supplicant woman raises a man's blood so that he wants to hit harder, rape more. She would have to think of some other way out of the bitterness. Tomorrow would bring its fresh store of bitterness, and the day after tomorrow yet a greater, but she would have to endure. The sobbing could not be in the open, only in the Women's Room. Meanwhile, she would write to "Agony Aunt Aggie" of *The Evening Star*. She would end her letter with, "Please advise me, but please don't advise me to give up my job, because my husband who is at present unemployed gets violent every time we have money problems and also because I have a three-year-old son who was born with a defective heart and who will need a very expensive operation."

"Helen, would you please come in for a minute? And bring the Meyer file."

"Yes, Mr Ong."

III
Bina

Woman, know that if you are a subject race socially, you move in the ancient literatures with the nobility and dignity of godlike spirits.
Know that your womanhood has been held as sacred among the Athapascans and the Anatolians, among the Chinese and the Chibcha, among the Irish and Iroquois, among the Japanese and the Jicarilla, among the Egyptians and the Eskimos, among the Mashona and the Mexicans, among the Semites and the Scandinavians, among the Zulu and the Zuni.
Woman, know this: that you hold up half the sky.

(From ***TWBOS****)*

Bina, her baby sister on her hip, was nevertheless able to manage the twenty skips, and so claim the prize which was the skipping rope itself, a length of hemp rescued from the garbage bin outside old Abu's shop. Her two friends, Fatimah and Zakira who had been turning the rope and counting in perfect unison, "One, two, three, four –", graciously handed over the prize which Bina expertly coiled and prepared to take home, to save against any future need. Meanwhile, she let her baby sister play with it, setting the baby on the hard earth of the playground, under a tree, where it sat contentedly chewing one end of the rope.

"I could do thirty skips if I wanted to," she said with happy confidence, adjusting her blouse which was held together in front by a row of safety pins, as well as the skirt which was too long and rimmed by dirt where it touched the ground.

"Is it true that you are going to be married soon?"

"Will your husband take you away, like Khalida's?"

The two interrogators, with solemn faces, faced Bina solicitously, touched by a sense of her tragedy and their own impending loss. For who could be a more wonderful playmate than Bina who skipped better than anyone, told stories and was ready to share her possessions? Once Bina saw a rupee at the bottom of a dried up well, in a clump of grass. She slid down, agile as a monkey, picked up the coin and clambered up, announcing the treasure and sharing it. Another day, she found a pencil, almost new, in old Abu's garbage bin. Old Abu provided good things in his overflowing bins and good stuff for gossip in his odd ways: it was rumoured in the village that he went to a beautiful woman in the darkness of night and then discovered the next morning that she was a leper. The frantic preventive treatment by the village doctor had cost him hundreds of rupees.

"You are going to be married. Your mother told our mother." They dealt out, sadly, the confirmation of her fate.

"I need not be married if I don't want to!" cried Bina with a defiant toss of her head. The sheer impossibility of this claim left her two friends speechless, and they gaped at her. Their turn would come too, they knew, if the Arab men asked for them and offered their parents good bride money. Khalidah fetched one thousand dollars, and Fauziah before her, only eight hundred, because she was darker. The men, they were told, liked their brides fair-complexioned.

"Keep away from the sun," admonished a hopeful mother and, to reinforce Nature's largesse, applied fine white powder liberally on the face of her twelve-year old, preparatory to the line-up of daughters for the inspection. In Bina's case, Nature's munificence to her parents had thrown up a startlingly fair child amidst a brood of dusky daughters; she had, moreover, a face like a doll's, hair like heavy jet curtains, and breasts which though as yet no more than buds under her thin cotton blouse, had the promise of full-blown fruit within the year. Her price would definitely be more than a thousand dollars, maybe one thousand five hundred, maybe even two thousand – who knows? Her father's hopes settled on this precious daughter. Soon the Arab men would be coming; his hopes soared.

"I don't want to be married," cried Bina and now her large doll's eyes were two limpid pools of terror, for she had heard the whispers, after Khalidah's wedding day, of how the girl had to be rushed, torn and bleeding and hysterical, to the hospital. They were whispers only, started by the women and ending with them, with no risk of their ever being blown into a village controversy that would invariably involve the men: the men did not want controversy to put an end to a highly lucrative practice by which daughters converted into hard cash that in turn converted into immediate businesses, motor cycles, dowries for other daughters, educational opportunities for sons, food for the whole family for years to come. Bina, with her astonishing beauty and promise of more beauty, was all these. Already a courier, acting for a very wealthy Arab, had expressed interest, and the Arab himself was coming to see with his own eyes, before the final offer.

The picture of Khalidah bleeding in 'the secret place' swam into Bina's mind with frightening vividness, blending with the picture of a rag doll she had once, torn into two between the legs where her sister had tried to wrench it away, so that the stuff inside its body spilled out, making it limp and lifeless.

"I don't want to be married!" The cry had lost its defiance; it was now all frantic pleading, and the two interrogators who had started it all, suddenly lost their nerve and turned to run away, just in time to escape blame, for Bina's mother appeared suddenly, looking very hot and cross.

"So there you are!" she scolded. "I've been looking everywhere for you. Where's Ameena? Oh my God, she's eating dirt. How irresponsible you are, Bina! But quick, come home now. Quick!" She picked up the baby and pushed Bina in the direction of home, all the time shrilly scolding, "I told you, didn't I, that today was the day, and you were not supposed to go anywhere and get all hot and dirty. Look at you! They'll be here in half an hour, Father says. Oh child, why do you always give your mother so much trouble?" The mother, thirty-two, had the furrowed brow of an old woman.

In half an hour Bina was ready. The mother smiled through her furrows of care to remark, "My child, God has given you so much beauty. Thank God for his blessings." She looked with pride at her daughter standing docilely in front of her; bathed, scrubbed, talcumed, wearing a new blouse and skirt, her hair properly oiled and coiled and decorated with a cluster of fragrant jasmine, her large eyes kohled to immense dark and luminous pools, and a little gold ring attached to her nose, she looked every inch the Child Goddess.

Her father said, "Two thousand, no less," and severely warned the mother, "and don't you appear too eager." He was a peanut vendor, plying his trade in the dusty streets of the nearby town, saved from despair by the sudden and tantalising prospect of large and immediate profits that had nothing to do with peanuts. He watched the Arabs making their shrewd reconnaissance surveys in his village and the villages around, their white flowing robes hiding corrupt, corpulent flesh, and he prepared to match them, skill for bargaining skill.

Looking at his daughter standing demurely with her eyes on the ground, he mentally adjusted the asking price to make it commensurate with her rare beauty, and looking at the prospective son-in-law, a sixty-five-year-old Arab so corpulent he had to be helped, wheezing, in and out of the chair, he adjusted the price further. The old man, slumped in the chair, his soft dimpled hands folded tranquilly upon his enormous belly, looked at the three girls ranged before him, their heads bowed, and, as everyone had expected, instantly picked Bina, indicating his preference by a slight movement of his forefinger.

"That one," he rasped, "and tell her to look up, I want to see her face," upon which Bina's father rapped out an order and she looked up. The Arab frowned, the mother gasped and let out a little scream, for they looked upon a contorted visage, eyes crossed horribly, mouth twisted grotesquely, and, for good measure, one cheek smudged black by a quick upward movement of the hand. The father shouted angrily, the mother ran up and shook the features back into normality, at the same time scrubbing out the smudge with one end of her sari. Bina, her stratagem of escape thus foiled, settled back into mute sullenness.

The Arab laughed. "I like her spirit," he said, and laughed again, this time in anticipation of the pleasure from that young, beautiful, vibrant body.

"She's too thin," he said, for he liked his females both fair and plump. "Feed her well, I'll be back in six months," and he got up to go, his huge bulk disengaged from the chair by three pairs of helping hands. He threw some money at the father. "For her," he said, "remember to feed her well. I come again in six months."

In six months he was back. Bina was two inches taller, ten pounds heavier. She stood before him, dressed in a pink satin blouse and red satin skirt, a veil over her head, radiating so much health and beauty that he was almost moved to tears.

The wedding was fixed for the following week. It was one of the most memorable events in the village for its lavishness, for the old Arab, thoroughly pleased with the bride whom he was going to take home with him the next day, spared no expense. At the wedding, fathers compared daughter prices: none matched Bina's and her father was pronounced the luckiest man and her mother the luckiest woman, for from the abundance accruing to the father (who was able to pay the deposit for a sweets business) was allowed her a gold nose ornament which she proudly wore for all the neighbors to see.

At the wedding, the bride, all the time she was sitting down and looking at her hands spread demurely on her knees, thought feverishly about what else she might do, having failed in the Ugly Face ploy. She kept thinking of Khalidah and the rag doll and went cold in her terror.

In the hotel room where their trunks were packed in readiness for the flight the next morning, she stood in a corner, still in her bridal clothes, staring miserably at him, the tears flowing freely. He, sitting in a chair, watched her, his face creased with extravagant good humour.

"Come, little one. Do not be afraid," he rasped. "Come. Do not cry."

She continued standing in her corner, the kohl causing little runnels of black down her cheeks. The sight of the girl, in her bridal finery, her small taut body poised for flight but held still by his mesmerizing power of proprietorship as he sat facing her, stirred his long dormant body to level after level of unexpected energy, surprising himself so that the excitation was both of flesh and spirit. He was monitoring his own bodily stirrings, as much as hers as she began to fidget in her corner, and was intrigued by both. He would wait a while longer, for waiting yielded immense dividends of pleasure.

So with languorous ease, he watched her from his chair, realising that this was the first time he had the chance for a long, uninterrupted and unobstructed view of her budding beauty: he watched her mouth, young and red and just now splendid in its tremulousness, her breasts which he thought, with self-congratulatory warmth, were the result of the good plentiful food he had ordered, her arms and her thighs, nurtured to the same firm, smooth, shiny roundness by the food.

He held out his hand gently to her and said, laughing, "Come, my little wife. Come to me, your husband."

"You can't sleep with me. I've got a disease!" cried Bina suddenly.

"Eh, what did you say?" cried the old Arab, delighted by this first attempt at communication by the child.

"You can't sleep with me because I've got leprosy, like Abu's woman," said Bina.

The Arab, puzzled, said, "Eh, you what?" and Bina, in a rush of hope, exclaimed breathlessly, "I've got leprosy! When a woman has leprosy, she cannot sleep with a man. Abu slept with a woman who had leprosy all over her body, but he did not know and he –" she dismissed from her mind the picture of Old Abu, strong and healthy in his sixtieth year and replaced it with that of a corpse, "died, because no doctor could cure him."

The Arab, smiling through this charming recital, said, when she had stopped speaking and was panting and twisting a corner of her bridal veil in her extreme nervousness, "Ah, so you have leprosy, my dear. But how is it you look so pretty, my dear?"

"It's all over my body, where you can't see it," cried Bina desperately.

"Ah, show it to me then!" cried her husband. "Show your pretty leprosy to me!"

By now the combined effects of the child-like banter, the sense of complete possession and privacy afforded by the locked hotel room, and the stimulus of the girl's mention of her own body, brought about such an access of pure animal energy that he sprang up from his chair, totally unaided, rushed upon her and dragged her to the bed. She hit out wildly, kicked, flailed, but he pinned her down easily with his whiskery face, his breath, his corpulence, silencing her at last with a stern, "Now stop that, or I shall tell your father." His soft dimpled hands were incapable of beating or slapping, so he threatened punishment from others acting on his behalf, whether fathers or guards. She quietened down and lay still, pinned under him, her eyes staring wildly.

"That's better," he grunted and proceeded to undress her, first the blouse and the vest under it, gaping in awe at the small, firm breasts, the nipples erect in terror, not expectation.

"Ah!" he rasped, and he 'ah'ed' all the way down, as his fingers, trembling with joy, undid the belt, the skirt and last of all the underpants. Like the glutton that saves the best for the last, he ignored the prize and instead began nuzzling upwards, beginning with the girl's belly, smooth as cream, and working the hoary bristles and wet old mouth towards her midriff, her breasts, her neck and finally her mouth. The girl, sick with fear, did nothing and said nothing, only making little noises like a small trapped animal, but at the moment when, in a brutal roar of release, he plunged into her and broke her, she screamed in the extremity of the pain and fear, her cry mixing with his in a simultaneous climax of man's doing and woman's receiving. If she had received a hundred scorpions, Bina would not have screamed in greater agony.

"Sssh, there now, not so much noise," panted the husband, and he rolled off her and settled beside her on the bed, a mountain of soft flesh, quivering in contentment. He lay for a while, then raised himself on his elbow to peer into her face and slap it lightly with his fingers, saying, "There, there, you're all right, wake up," for she had fainted.

He lay for a long while, his whole person suffused by a delicious ease. Never had he felt so fulfilled. If he were not so out of breath, he would have got up to do a celebratory jig, so happy was he. To think he had believed his ability was lost forever! No doctor was now needed, only this young, beautiful bride he was going to take home with him. The vision of limbs, firm, supple, luscious, interlaced with his, multiplied in an endlessly stretching vista of pleasure down the years. He was to die, literally, in the throes of his lust, his huge, inert bulk pulled away from the poor little whimpering body under it by his two guards who had heard the child's cries for help. But it was not Bina; it was another Indian girl brought over from another village, after a few years of his lying low. For what had happened was that Bina, in the plane to her new home, had plucked up enough courage, when her husband had fallen asleep, to tug at the hand of the air stewardess and draw attention to her plight. Her Ugly Face ploy and Leprosy ploy having failed, this third attempt at self-rescue worked. The stewardess swung into a high drama of rescue, and the story made headlines around the world: 'Child Bride Rescued', 'Girl, 11, sold in Marriage to 65-year-old Man,' 'The Two-thousand-dollar Child Bride.' Highly embarrassed, the authorities did the needful – the girl was put into state custody; the Arab was disgraced, warned and sent home; the stewardess was commended and promoted and a team of Government officials descended upon Bina's village to 'investigate' and write a report, sending fathers and marriage middlemen into hiding. Three people offered to adopt Bina, including the air stewardess and a well-known Indian feminist; her father, terrified by the publicity, tearfully offered to return every cent of the money to have his daughter back. But it was in the state interest to have Bina in state custody, and everything was promised to 'restore her dignity as a female and give her a proper education.'

The Child Bride Affair, as it was called died out after a while and was forgotten altogether in the new interest generated by an event in another part of the world, the United States of America, where a remarkable series of Senate hearings was set up to investigate accusations of sexual harassment made by a woman against the President's nominee for Supreme Court Judge. With or without the 'Judge Thomas Affair,' as it was called, the 'Child Bride Affair' would have died a natural death; as it turned out, it was easily consigned to oblivion by the authorities' regretful reminder that they could do nothing about such things since no formal complaints had been lodged. Hence 'such things' continued, and after a few years of lying low, the old Arab, unable to forget the extraordinary effect young bodies had on his, continued his search in the Indian villages and was able to take back not one, but several young girls, ending with the one on whom literally, as was earlier mentioned, he died in his last act of love. After Bina, he had had no more trouble, through the simple precaution of dispensing larger sums of bride money and enjoining, very sternly, upon the parents, the necessity of warning their daughters to shut up in planes, on pain of 'serious harm' to their families if they 'misbehaved.'

So, given stark poverty on the one side and flowing money on the other, the bride trade continues and Bina's little baby sister Ameena, just now toddling barefoot outside the house but already showing promise of the same startling beauty as her sister, will have to endure the same fate.

IV

The Paper Women

According to the Chinese, the Goddess Nu Kwa, during the time when the heavens and the earth shattered, quickly came to repair the damage, using coloured stones to patch up the skies and the four legs of the great turtle to support the earth. Indian records tell us that if the Goddess Devi were to close her eyes even for a second, the entire universe would disappear. According to the ancient Akkadians, it was the Goddess Mami who first placed life on earth, by pinching off fourteen pieces of clay, making seven of them into women, and seven into men. Mexican records tell of the Goddess Coatlicue, who gave birth to the moon, the sun and all other deities. The Australian Aborigines explain that it is to the Goddess Kunapipi that our spirits return upon death, remaining with her until the next rebirth.

The testimony to woman's power is for all time, whether scratched on clay, chiselled in stone, inked on silk or printed on paper.

(From **TWBOS***)*

An easy operation, my friend had said, by way of calming my fears, because I had confided in her the nightmares that started coming as soon as I had made the decision. That was about eight years ago. I saw myself sliced open and my women's fecundity, a bunch of soft golden eggs, pulled out and squelched up. I would wake up panting in terror and once woke Larry who stirred, grunted and rolled over to fit snugly into any receptive curve of my body, as he liked to do when asleep. I think I had six of these nightmares, each more horrendous than the last; in the final one, I hung, like a plucked chicken from the ceiling, my raw insides being slowly enticed out by gravitational suasion, until someone (a nurse, I think) walked by, looked up and matter-of-factly stuffed them back.

But the reality was far, far removed from the nightmare.

"You mean it's all over?" I asked. I was still groggy from the anaesthestics, but felt not the slightest pain.

"Yes, it's all over," smiled the nurse.

"Can I go home?" I asked.

"You need to rest a day here, and then you can be discharged," said the nurse.

Of course, Larry and I did not want to talk about the operation which could not have been a very comfortable subject for discussion, but we had talked, weeks before, of the subject that had made the operation necessary. It had begun with Meng's failing to get into the kindergarten of our choice, the best kindergarten in Singapore. Larry was furious. The principal had told him that Meng was one hundred and twenty-second on the waiting list. It was highly regrettable parental negligence not registering him in that kindergarten as soon as he was born. Now he was three, and it was too late.

"I don't want the same thing to happen to the boy when he reaches school-going age," said Larry grimly. I knew he had in mind the best primary boys' school in Singapore for which parents would have offered immense bribes, but since this was not one of the normal channels for cooperation, they had to resort to other measures.

The surest one was for the mother of the child to undergo sterilisation at a government hospital and produce proof thereof, upon which the school, having been previously briefed, would immediately enrol the child. This measure was in line with the government's goal to achieve national prosperity through strict population control: Singapore women were alarmingly fecund and Kandang Kerbau Maternity Hospital had the dubious distinction of registering one of the highest birth-rates in the world. A slew of birth control measures, including aggressive sloganeering, public haranguing, employment disincentives and income tax penalties, appeared not to work. Then somebody hit on the brilliant idea: if parents wanted to send their children to the established premier schools of Singapore, the mothers would have to produce sterilisation certificates. For Chinese parents put such a high premium on the education of their children, especially their sons, that they would be prepared to lose an arm and a leg to secure all the opportunities they could for the sons' advancement in this world. So what was the loss of a pair of ovaries? The population control policy worked like a dream.

I handed over a copy of the sterilisation certificate to the school principal, Larry was very pleased, and our son Meng got into an excellent school of our choice where he did extremely well so that each time he came back with school prizes and glowing report cards, Larry beamed and patted him and gave him expensive presents, while I congratulated myself on the wisdom of my decision.

I wished, though, that other problems in our marriage could have been just as easily solved. Consider: Husband gets angry because Wife is showing too much interest in her career. Wife goes for operation to remove 'Career Gland'. Husband complains Wife does not love him. Wife goes for operation to put in 'Love Husband' gland.

There is no point going into the problems now. They are so complex and yet seem no more than accumulations of the most appalling trivia that they defy analysis. It is best to cut through this marital Gordian knot by simply settling on incompatibility. About ten years after the operation, when I was thirty six, we decided that things were not going too well and like many couples before us, we thought to give our marriage a second chance by going on this extended holiday, sometimes coyly referred to as the 'second honeymoon'.

A tour of Bangkok and Manila could be managed despite our busy work schedules; Larry got 'special' leave from his company (he said his boss was very understanding) and I managed to get what is known as 'no pay leave' from my company.

Now I confess, to my embarrassment, that the holiday did not have the desired effect and that shortly after we returned, we decided to separate. I further confess, with some self-reproach, that in spite of the very lavish treatment during the ten days of the tour – Larry took me to the best hotels, most expensive restaurants, most exclusive shopping areas in a frenzy of spending to reclaim lost marital ground – I remember nothing of this second honeymoon.

Except two small incidents, and very inconsequential ones, at that.

We were in a hotel in Bangkok, certainly one of the best in the city and one highly recommended by a business associate of Larry's. Alas for the futility of a hotel's expenditure of effort and money upon indifferent guests like myself! I sat in a corner of the hotel foyer, absorbed in thought, waiting for Larry who was supposed to meet me there, impervious to the blandishments of hotel chandeliers and floral extravaganzas and thick carpets.

"Ma'am." The small voice made me turn round. I saw a young Thai girl standing in front of me and holding something out to me. It was a scrap of paper, a receipt, whatever, which must have dropped out of my handbag when I had earlier opened it to pull out a piece of tissue. She was a very pretty girl, about fourteen or fifteen at the most. I took the piece of paper from her and was wondering whether to offer her some money and how much, when she turned and walked back to join a small cluster of young-looking girls like herself sitting quietly in a corner. They looked like they were getting ready to go on a trip, and waiting for someone to herd them into a bus or van. They all had the lustrous eyes and hair and burnished skins for which Thai women are famous.

"Who are they?" I asked one of the hotel attendants, a young man who called himself 'Tommy', spoke good English and seemed more sociable than the rest.

"Virgins," he said. "Virgin prostitutes. With good proof. Their price is much higher."

I puzzled over the contradiction in terms.

"Where are they going?" I asked.

"To Hong Kong," he said "The next group arrives this evening, to replace them." I would have liked to know more but decided not to engage the friendly, young man in conversation that could prove embarrassing. Besides, Larry would not approve. I remembered that Grandfather, when he was already seventy-two, still demanded virgins from the pool of bondmaids in Grandmother's household, for the act of defloration conferred upon an aging man great powers so that he rose from the de-virginised body revitalised.

I saw the girls being herded into one of the hotel vans by a tall dark man. The girl who had returned me the receipt saw me, smiled and gave me a look which I returned – a strange look that established, in some indefinable way, a small bond of affinity that said, "We are going to meet again."

I did not tell Larry about the Virgin Prostitutes.

"Ma'am." It would appear I had got into the habit of dropping things from my handbag. This time it was in Manila, in a busy shopping centre. The woman who was probably in her twenties had one child on her hip and another by the hand, and it was this child who, prompted by the mother, shyly held out the air ticket I had dropped. Larry was aghast at my carelessness; he took over the air ticket for safekeeping in his wallet. I gave the child some money, and the mother smiled and began talking to me. "You from Singapore?" she said cheerfully. "I got a sister working in Singapore. She earns good money." Filipinas were pouring into Singapore to work as domestic servants, but not before they had given a written undertaking to the Government that they would not get pregnant.

I don't remember what I said to her, probably some inanity about the beauty of her country and the friendliness of the people. Then she gave me a look, and I swear it was that strange affinity-establishing look again which sent a little thrill through me.

"We are going to meet again," it said, and I said, "Yes," before Larry hustled me away. From that moment, the three of us had become curiously linked as a trio in my mind, three women who by no stretch of the imagination belonged together: myself, a thirty-seven year old woman executive from Singapore with a Master in Business Administration degree from British Columbia University, she, the child-woman prostitute working in a Bangkok hotel and the other she, a young housewife from Manila with two small children, envious of her sister who had come to Singapore to work as a maid.

"How was the second honeymoon?" The slyly good-natured question would have elicited a totally inappropriate reply: I met a little girl prostitute in Bangkok and a young Filipino mother in Manila, and now we seem to form a sisterhood and I am puzzled as to why.

The divorce was as amiable as any under the circumstances; we shared rights to Meng, for whose sake we had delayed the divorce until after he had finished the all important PSLE examinations which he passed with flying colours. Even before the divorce had come through, I was already seeing Y, and to this day, Y is branded by my family and Larry's as being the one single rogue factor in the otherwise happy equation of our marriage. I got the house, the car, a sizable bank account – but oh! I would have given up all these, indeed, ten times all these – if I could have got it back. But they said the operation was irreversible.

The puzzlement disappeared as soon as we met again, and I recognised both instantly. There we were, the three of us, in the clinic waiting for the doctor's nurse to call us, sitting facing each other, our respective pieces of paper in our hands. I with the Sterilisation Certificate, hoping against hope that it would not daunt this doctor from attempting to reverse the operation and give me back my womanhood, she, the Virgin Prostitute holding her Virginity Certificate and waiting for a renewal before starting work in a Singapore hotel, and the other she, holding the Certificate of Non-Pregnancy now invalidated by the small swell beginning to show and hoping that it would be sufficient justification for a quick abortion.

We were a band of women whose sexuality had been reduced to pieces of paper signed by men.

We are the Paper Women.

V

The Rest Is Bonus

It was thanks to the Goddess Ukemochi that the people of Japan always had food to eat, for from her came the abundance of the rice in the fields, the animals in the mountains and the fish of the rivers and seas. One day, the great Amaterasu sent her brother, the moon God Tsuki Yomi, to serve Ukemochi in her heavenly palace. Now this was a great insult to his pride. Arriving at Ukemochi's palace, he was presented with rice, fish and meat in a great banquet, but he refused the food, insisting that Ukemochi had vomited it out of her own body. Then his anger became very great indeed and he took out his sword and murdered the Goddess Ukemochi. So gentle and magnanimous was the goddess that even as she lay in death, she continued to bless him with abundance: from her stomach came rich harvests of rice, from her head came horses and oxen, from the black silk of her eyebrows came the threads for the weaving looms. When the Great Amaterasu heard of the murder, she was filled with rage against her evil brother and banished him from the heavens. He began to be ashamed of himself, and repented so deeply of the dishonour of his act that he remained hidden in his shame.

*(From **TWBOS**)*

It was the last peaceful hour of the day for the family before the quiet of the vast rubber plantation would be shattered by the drunken roaring of the father on his way home from the town, the roar swelling to the preternatural howl of the doomed beast if he happened, in his crazed plunge through the dark forest, to hit his head against a tree trunk or drive his foot through a sharp root. But the hour of the father's coming was not yet, so the mother and children could still be together, sitting quietly on the cool cement pavement outside their house, one in a long row of low wooden huts. Once painted a bright yellow to lend some domestic cheer to the grim lives of their inhabitants, the rubber tappers making their endless rounds in that vast implacable interior, they had lost the brightness and now stood in the dereliction of peeling paint, broken shutters, and faecal smudges left by children's hands.

In the dim light cast out by the one unshaded bulb in the house, Meenachi and her six children huddled together, waiting. The growing hunger for the one meal of the day, clumps of curried rice washed over with milk, laid out on banana leaves on the floor but forbidden to all to touch until the father came home, caused the group to unhuddle and disperse, to look around for something to do, so as to distract themselves from the hunger. The three small boys, all with shaved heads to make for easier application of ointment on persistent scalp boils, and all with very hard, round stomachs above their tattered khaki shorts, wandered off and soon returned with an unripe jackfruit which they tried to prise open; the eldest, a girl named Letchmy, aged ten, had pulled out a plastic doll with one eye from under her blouse and was rocking it in her arms; the younger girl, a small skeletal child with matted hair, was unsteadily walking around a sleeping cat and prodding it with a twig, and the youngest child, a baby, naked except for a dirt-encrusted string around its buttocks, was crawling towards something with investigative interest.

Meenachi sat on the ground and leaned against the doorpost, dreaming of a nose stud which she had once seen in a goldsmith's shop on one of the very rare trips to town: it was the most beautiful nose-stud she had ever seen, a rich red gem set in gold. She pictured it in all its resplendence, securely fastened on her nose above the left nostril.

Nose-stud vanished in the reality of head-lice: her daughter Letchmy, still carrying the doll, drew near for the regular exercise of de-lousing, lowering her head for her mother's deft fingers to search her hair, pull out each hidden denizen and expertly crush it between thumb and forefinger. Then it was the mother's turn to unloose her large knot of hair and spread out the long, dark strands for the daughter's fingers to sweep through. It was an exercise of mutual comfort, and Meenachi once more leaned back, closed her eyes and dreamed, as Letchmy, with small, eager cries, kept count of her catch.

Nose-stud and head-lice vanished in the greater urgency of food: the baby, unseen by anyone, had crawled into the house towards the dinner on the banana leaves and was now sitting on it and eating it in fistfuls. Meenachi shouted, scrambled up and rushed to rescue the food, and it was in the midst of the pandemonium of the mother shrilly scolding, the baby screaming and the rest of the children crying over the despoiled dinner that the father appeared, unannounced. He stood at the doorway, one hand on the doorpost to steady himself, his blood-shot eyes trying to take in the meaning of this unwonted scene, his huge, glistening chest heaving with ominous energy. The noise stopped immediately, and a circle of pale frightened faces turned towards him.

That was all that was needed to trigger an explosion of that terrible energy: a tremendous roar and a huge fist raised to strike sent the children scattering in all directions, Letchmy adroitly pulling the baby up from the floor with one arm and grabbing her little sister with the other, leaving the mother alone to meet the impact of the hurtling fist. It crashed into her left cheek, then her left eye and sent her reeling to one end of the room where she hit the wall and slid down to the floor in a crumbled heap, crying softly, her long hair plastered to her wet face.

"Ai-yoooh! Ai-yoooh!" moaned Meenachi.

Her husband, his breath coming out in short, sharp rasps, his fists still clenched with unspent fury, stood over her. She should have thought better than to moan; piteous sounds of supplication, like terror-stricken looks on faces, only goaded him to greater fury. He lifted a foot and dealt her a kick which sent her body skidding crazily across the now wet floor. Her cries subsiding to a thin, almost inaudible wail, she put her arms tightly around her belly and pulled up her legs around it in further protection, like the jungle creature that curls up into a tight ball in an encounter with the enemy.

The sight of his wife thus curled up in self-protection

had the effect of a gesture of open defiance; with another roar he rushed upon her to smash at that defiance, forcing open her arms and legs. Her blouse, held together by three safety pins, burst open, flinging out her breasts and her sarong ripped to expose her nakedness.

"Aaarh-rh!" he roared, and the violence of attack became one with the violence of sex, so that the pain of his fist upon her face and his foot upon her head was one with the pain of his thrusting ferocity between her legs.

She did not dare tell him that she was pregnant.

He was soon asleep, snoring and slobbering on her in his drunken wetness.

Raising her head slightly, she saw the frightened faces of her children at the doorway, and silently signalled to them to come in. She then eased her body out from under his, taking care not to wake him, stood up, adjusted her clothes and got ready to feed her children with whatever could be saved from their dinner.

The goddess with the kind smile was her hope. In the morning when her husband had left for work, she gave instructions for Letchmy to take care of the other children, and with her offerings wrapped in a piece of cloth, she stole out of the house to the shrine, a small stone structure on the edge of the plantation where the goddess, no bigger than a doll but imposing in the wisdom of her enormous eyes and full breasts, and in the proliferation of flower and silver tinsel garlands round her neck, stood with one arm raised in blessing. Meenachi tremblingly undid the cloth bundle and brought out half a coconut, and some flowers which she arranged carefully at the feet of the goddess. Bowing her head in deepest supplication, she told the goddess of her troubles and begged for her help.

And this was what she told the goddess: her husband got drunk and beat her every day of the week. He smashed things in the house; there was no unbroken cup or saucer left and the pots and pans were dented and twisted beyond use. He wanted sex every day even when she was feeling very sick; her pregnancy this time was the worst and she felt sick all the time. He wanted sex with his daughter Letchmy whenever he was drunk. So far she had succeeded in getting the child out of the way, but she was not sure she could go on doing that much longer.

Meenachi's litany of sorrows ended with her lighting a cloth wick in a small saucer of coconut oil, and raising it in final pleading with the goddess. She longed for a sign. If at that moment, a wind had arisen and swooshed around the stone statue, or a petal had suddenly detached itself and floated away or a bird alighted near the offerings, that would have constituted a divine promise of intervention to check her husband's excesses. But the goddess, resplendent in her green, pink and purple paint and load of tinsel garlands, gave no such sign, only continuing to smile benignly.

Meenachi, parting the tangled masses of hair from her face to place the lit wick at the feet of the goddess, refused to be discouraged. Suddenly struck by an idea which gathered the sorrowfulness in her eyes into a look of clear purpose, she said: "Most merciful goddess, if you see fit not to do anything, I will understand and will still come with these humble offerings. If, however, you will be so kind as to take pity on me and do something to help me,

I will return with better offerings – a full coconut, not this wretched half." A coconut cost money, unless she searched the grass in the nearby coconut plantation for any that had fallen, but she was reckless with the need to complete the bargain with the goddess.

She looked beseechingly into the purple and pink face and thought she saw a smile of approval.

"I shall come back in a week," said Meenachi, carrying the negotiations to a further stage by shrewdly setting a deadline for the goddess.

"One week," repeated Meenachi, whose conceptualisation of time was always in terms of this unit, it being the basis for the paying out of wages on the rubber plantation and hence the chief regulating force of husbands' moods: husbands beat wives more frequently towards the end of pay-week when the money had run out and no more trips could be made to the toddy bars in the town.

That night, a Tuesday and pay-day, her husband came back more drunk than usual, as expected. He slumped into a chair, eyes closed, then roared for his daughter Letchmy who had, in anticipation, gone to hide in a neighbour's house. The sex after the beating was more painful than usual, as the pregnancy was proving to be unbearable; she begged to be allowed to get up, but he restrained her, laughing. She managed to slip away when he dropped off to sleep at last, and was violently sick as she squatted over the drain outside the house. On Thursday, he hit her on the spot where a swelling from a previous punch had barely subsided but with a mixture of mashed wild forest plants and coconut oil, she was able to get the swelling down. On Friday, the beating was after the sex, when he wanted more and she demurred, and he pulled her towards him by her hair and then slapped her. Two teeth were punched out on Sunday when she came to the protection of one of the boys who had annoyed the father but was able to wriggle himself free and run away.

Tuesday came round again, and with it, the visit to the goddess's shrine, as agreed on. Meenachi, nursing a bruised eye, hurried out of the house with her cloth bundle of offerings. She fell at the feet of the goddess and opened the bundle, revealing a very large coconut, whole not half.

"Thank you, Goddess," she breathed in the fullness of gratitude. "Thank you for helping me." For during the week she had been hit only four days, not the full seven, a tremendous improvement, and besides, the hitting had not been on the belly, not even once, but only on the other parts of her body. Best of all, her daughter Letchmy had gone to stay with the neighbour's mother, a kindly old woman who lived in the town, so that was one big source of worry out of the way. She aggregated her gains – three full days without any beating. A substantial bonus indeed, for which she was deeply grateful.

"Thank you, Goddess," she said again, and with the same shrewdness of the week before, she added, "Please continue to help me and lessen my troubles. Next week I shall come again and maybe this time I will be able to bring a better offering than this humble coconut, maybe even a –" Meenachi did not want to commit herself to such an expensive gift but it came out, "garland." Garlands were unaffordable, but her recklessness grew with the conviction of the goddess's growing concern for her.

That night nothing happened; her husband though drunk, went to sleep peacefully, and the next night, still nothing happened. There was only one moment of anxiety when he suddenly roused himself from his stupor to ask for his daughter. She told him where the girl was, trembling in her nervousness and readying her body for blows, but instead the man became all sentimental and maudlin, calling upon God to bear witness to his love for his child, bemoaning his unhappy life and wiping off the tears in his eyes with the back of his hand. He fell asleep soon afterwards, snoring loudly. Two nights later, the destructive energy reasserted itself fully: he bellowed his way home through the dark plantation, plunging through the trees with ferocious impatience to reach home and vent that energy.

The cause this time was a secret raging anger against larger forces beyond his control. There had been rumours of retrenchment because of the declining price of natural rubber brought on by new claims of synthetic, and he knew, from the general hostility of the plantation superintendent towards him, that he would be among the first to go. He tried to forget his fear and anger in drink, but by the time he staggered out of the toddy bar, neither had disappeared, and he was soon on his way home to make sure they were properly discharged. Several of the children who got in his way were thrashed, but Meenachi bore the full brunt of it. He sent her flying to the end of the room; she was too preoccupied with staunching the flow of blood from a reopened wound on the cheek, to remember to clasp her belly tightly and curl up into the protective enfoldment of arms and legs, so that the next moment he was kicking her all over her body. He watched her writhing and moaning on the floor, his muscles rippling with ancient hates and lusts.

Then she stopped moaning and lay very still. He bent down, peered at her and dealt a few vigorous slaps on her cheeks to wake her up, but when she continued to be totally motionless, he took fright, ran to the bathroom, came out with a bucket of water and splashed her face with it. Still she did not move, and then he noticed a pool of blood under her which was spreading outwards. He became panic-stricken, running hither and thither, clasping his head in his hands and blubbering in his indecisiveness. The hostile, hateful face of the superintendent loomed before his eyes and added to his panic: if the enemy should come to know that he was responsible for his wife's death, there would be no end of trouble for him. The prospect of prison was frightening.

"Meenachi!" he yelled, shaking her by the shoulder. She stirred, and an eyelid opened.

"Meenachi, don't die!" He laid her head on his lap and began rocking her gently, but she had lapsed into unconsciousness once more.

* * *

"Forgive me, dear goddess," said Meenachi at the shrine, two weeks later, still looking pale but otherwise recovered from her miscarriage, "for not keeping the appointment, but I was in hospital and was only discharged yesterday." It was redundant information to an all-knowing deity, but deference required it. She had with her a large brown paper package which she now placed before the goddess with trembling self-consciousness.

"See, you have kept your promise, and so I have kept mine," she said, smiling with growing pleasure as her fingers pulled out a garland of jasmine and gold tinsel and put it reverently round the neck of the stone statue, on top of heaps of the other garlands, but all definitely inferior.

The garland had been bought for her by her husband in an uninterrupted flow of amiability since her being rushed to the hospital in an ambulance. He had hovered by her bedside, had been visibly nervous when he heard her being questioned by the hospital authorities about her miscarriage and the various bruises and swellings on her body, and had at last heaved an immense sigh of relief when she explained everything in terms of her general carelessness when moving about in the house doing housework so that knocks and bruises and other injuries were now second nature. She exceeded her husband's expectations when, in reply to a blunt question by a skeptical nurse, she said that her husband had never laid a finger on her once in her life. He, too, on his part exceeded her expectations, indeed, to such a degree that she was now breathless in her impatience to tell all to the goddess.

"Thank you, Goddess, for it must be owing to you that he gave me this," she cried, pointing, not to the broken nose but the nose-stud sitting unsteadily on it.

"Oh, Goddess, thank you!" She had with her a small broken piece of mirror which she carried in a fold of her sarong, to provide the continuous pleasure of gazing at the beautiful red gem set in gold, nestling precariously on the nose not yet healed, a bonus breathtaking in its munificence.

VI

The Song Of Golden Frond

"... to teach in song the lessons you have learned in suffering."

(From ***TWBOS****)*

Golden Frond who died more than forty years ago sang a joyous song because she was special.

She was left on Grandmother's doorstep when she was three by a very frightened woman who was either her mother or kidnapper; the woman asked for the promised money and left quickly. Grandmother brought the child into the house and scrutinised her closely, noting the scabs on her head in between the poor tufts of hair, the swollen belly, the legs crooked from malnutrition. The child stared at Grandmother, biting a corner of her dress. She had no knickers. Grandmother was not daunted. Proper food, regular baths, large doses of her home-made brews to de-worm even the most infested stomachs: the transformation could be startling so that within a year, the child would no longer be recognisable. The evidence was there in the semicircle of her healthy-looking girls of varying ages, just now watching and giggling at the newcomer: in their time, their scabs and lice and worms had disappeared under Grandmother's capable hands. Grandmother had a household of eight bondmaids then, the most skilful being put to work in her business of making hand-sewn beaded bridal slippers, and the rest to all manner of household work. As the older ones left to be married off, Grandmother replenished the supply of labour by taking in new ones, the youngest acceptable age being about that of Golden Frond, as Grandmother had no patience with babies.

But that was not yet her name when she appeared before Grandmother and the semicircle of giggling fellow bondmaids.

"Dustbin."

"Dumb. Call her 'Dumb'. She has not answered any of our questions."

"Bad smell."

The bondmaids, when they were sold into the household, were given new names, but not nearly as humble: 'Pig', 'Prawn', 'Wind-in-the-Head', 'Female'.

"My name is to be Golden Frond."

The sheer audacity of the claim, lisped through lips still rimmed with snot and dirt, was not without its appeal. Grandmother, taken aback, laughed. Her laughter being a most rare departure from a severity of mien all the more fearsome because it always preceded a resounding knock on the head with powerful knuckles, the bondmaids quickly took advantage of it, and laughed in their turn.

"And why is your name to be Golden Frond?"

For answer, the child broke into song, her voice a pitiful little quaver, accompanying her words with well-rehearsed clapping and stamping motions. She stopped, stared at the audience, and when nothing happened and nobody came forward with money or food, she began to recite a poem or bits of poems put together, and when still nothing happened, in desperation the child lifted her dress, waggled her bottom and gathered her lips into a soft flower bud for a kiss, completing the 'Bad Woman' routine.

Grandmother laughed again, shaking her head.

Golden Frond was allowed to keep her name and over the years rose in beauty to match the splendour of that name while the others correspondingly sank to match the grossness of theirs: Golden Frond, like a bright-faced, slender-limbed goddess moved among a brood of squat, snub-nosed peasant girls with names redolent of rice fields, latrines and life's meanness.

Some suspicion attached to her unusual beauty, especially her very fair complexion and curling hair.

"*Serani*," the bondmaids whispered. There was probably some Eurasian blood in the child; Grandmother once told the story of a village woman whose child was born with blue eyes and was immediately given away.

Golden Frond, thus special, stood apart from the rest. When she was five, she was put to simple tasks such as separating out the bridal slipper beads according to size or colour. Sometimes she nodded over the little piles of beads but was jerked awake by Grandmother's knuckles on her head, but mostly she completed her work well and did not make mistakes.

When Golden Frond was five years old, Grandfather was sixty, First Uncle, Grandfather's firstborn, was thirty-eight and First Uncle's firstborn, Older Cousin, was thirteen.

Golden Frond's work, at five years, was to serve the three men in the household in the following ways: in the morning, she listened for the first sounds of Grandfather's waking up, crackling sounds of a prolonged and laboured clearing of early morning phlegm from the throat. She then brought up to his room a tray with a mug of hot tea and a hot face towel. She would wait for Grandfather to finish drinking the tea and wiping his face, neck and armpits and then take the empty mug and used towel downstairs. The same routine was followed for First Uncle whose room was just across the corridor; the alerting sound in this case was the gush of morning piss into the chamberpot. Golden Frond listened for the last hiss, then went up with the tea and towel. There was an extra towel for Older Cousin who shared the room with his father. In the evening, Golden Frond took up two chamberpots, one for each of the rooms, in readiness for the night. She could manage only one chamberpot at a time, and once, she dropped the large enamel utensil, which went clanging all the way downstairs. She watched, frightened, as it finally settled at the bottom of the stairs, badly dented. Fortunately, Grandmother was not at home at the time, and the bondmaid called 'Pig', who did not like her, said, "I'll tell Grandmother when she comes back, and she will give you more knocks on your head and pinches on your thighs!"

At five, she was too young to carry the filled, sometimes overbrimming pots down the long flight of steps in the morning, and an older bondmaid was assigned the duty, but when she reached the age of eleven, the duty fell on her. Her beauty was already conspicuous at that age and visitors, watching her arrange beads or cut paper patterns would say to Grandmother in a whisper, "That child's very pretty. She looks different from the others," and Grandmother would say, "Ssh. Don't put ideas in her head. She has to earn her keep like everybody else."

When Golden Frond was eleven years old, Grandfather was sixty-six, First Uncle was forty-four and Older Cousin was nineteen.

"Come. Come here."

The young man who had been watching the child all the while that she was carrying the chamberpot to his room and placing it carefully on a little square of mat, sat on the edge of his bed with his fat legs wide apart and a smile playing on his face. He had been handsome only up to his fifteenth year and then an illness which no amount of help from the temple mediums had been able to cure, blew his body up into grotesque proportions and sank his eyes into appalling cushions of fat. Some said his brains too had been softened by the illness which accounted for his odd behaviour. Grandmother had grimly sent for his mother (who had gone back to live with her own parents when Older Cousin was but a child), but the woman under one pretext or another put off the day of return, until Grandmother saw through her wiles and dismissed her completely from all family matters. "He has no mother; he is to be pitied," she would say.

"Come here."

Bondmaids never disobeyed masters, young or old.

His trousers were unbuttoned and he watched her, grinning. She stood facing him uncertainly, conscious that he was doing a bad thing and wanted her to be part of it.

"Come here!" His voice rose to an imperious shout; the grin disappeared in a rictus of pure annoyance.

At that moment, somebody from downstairs called her name and the child, unlocked from the terror, spun round and ran downstairs, and into a circle of light and loving in the centre of which was old Ah Por, her gentle protectress. Old Ah Por, almost blind, a mere wisp of a woman, was more spirit than flesh in the last years of her life spent in Grandmother's household. She was Grandmother's much revered half sister who had gone into a nunnery in China as a girl and then, in her old age, returned to die in the house where she had been born. She did not die till six years later, when Golden Frond had reached the age of seventeen, and during this time, the girl, put to the task of taking care of the old, half-blind, helpless woman, combing her hair, feeding her, massaging her legs with embrocation oil, felt the thrilling sense of being protected herself. Old Ah Por's presence threw a golden cordon of security against the menacing shadows around.

For the truth was that as she grew into womanhood, she felt the dark, turbulent world of Grandfather, First Uncle and Older Cousin with their incessant demands and appetites, closing in upon her, as it had already closed in upon her sister bondmaids, pulling them into its darkness.

One day, when she was about twelve, she passed

Grandfather's room and saw through the door that was only partially closed, Grandfather on the bed on top of the bondmaid Pig, Pig's trousers lying in a round heap on the floor and her waist-string a snake-coil on the heap, and a few days later, as she was walking down the stairs, she again caught a glimpse of Pig (or was it Bun?) being pulled into First Uncle's room and saw the door firmly closing upon them. Older Cousin, monstrously fat, prowled the house, sniffing and gurgling, wanting his rightful share of the spoils. Grandmother moved resignedly in this turbulent world of men and appetites not of her making.

"They are farmyard roosters, all," she said grimly by way of explanation, "that go mad with the smell of first blood. What do you expect of roosters in the midst of hens and pullets?"

The sinister shadows drew closer and were repelled by the radiance of Ah Por's gentle goodness, for Ah Por, incessantly praying to the deities, had become one herself. Still in this world but no longer of it, she spoke to Kuan Yin, Goddess of Mercy, as to an intimate. No meat touched her lips, in order to be worthy of the Goddess. Golden Frond loved to prepare her meals of rice porridge and soya bean curd, and get ready the joss sticks and flowers for her daily worship at the Goddess's altar. Upon this incense-filled world of the pure of heart, the tumult of blood and groin could not intrude, and so Golden Frond stayed close by the side of Old Ah Por. She could feel the heavy breathing of desire sometimes come very close, and hear the sharpness of thwarted desire in the men's curses upon a burst button or a missing penknife or soup that was too salty, men's curses ringing with the full scatology of the most private parts and odours of woman's body. Yet she felt safe and at ease, and sang a joyous song as she moved about in her duties.

When she was seventeen years old, Ah Por died. Golden Frond, returning with a warmed bowl of porridge, found her slumped in her chair, her spirit already flown, as she had so often intimated, to be with Kuan Yin.

Golden Frond wept, her heart breaking. Who was to protect her now? The world of the howling blackness would break upon her soon. This was when she had reached the age of seventeen; Grandfather was seventy-two, First Uncle was fifty and Older Cousin was twenty-five.

"Come here."

The old man's voice, firm and authoritative, came through the open door of his room as she was hurrying past. She stopped, head bowed, heart beating.

"Come here."

It turned out he only wanted the back-knocking.

"The weather's getting too cold," he said brusquely by way of explanation, without looking at her. Cold weather made old bones ache, so wives and bondmaids stood behind masters and gently knocked their backs with rhythmic small clenched fists until told to stop.

"Start," he said, turning his back to her, still not looking at her and continuing with the mixing of inks at his desk.

She knocked gently on his back, moving her small balled fists expertly up and down and across the broad expanse of his powerful back. The large, heavy clock on the wall ticked the minutes away. The back, under the impact of the diligently working fists, began to ripple with desire. The old man said, "Stop, that's enough," and swung round, and would have caught her by the wrist and pulled her to his bed, as he had done with innumerable bondmaids if a voice had not called then and saved her, a second time. It was not old Ah Por's voice, for that had been stilled forever and Ah Por's ashes now lay in an urn in the temple. It was the voice of a man, calling her. She was saved by a man.

He was a scholar cousin who had been invited into the household by Grandmother; they were told to call him Older Brother. He came with his crate of books, shortly after Ah Por's death and was given her room, still redolent of the joss fumes. He was gaunt, unsmiling, with the scholar's taciturnity and impatience with trifles. The bondmaids, their eyes lowered as they moved about, watched him closely and by the second week, were able to conclude that he was unlike the other three and would leave them alone. Indeed, they placed him squarely outside the generality of men: he showed kindness to women.

"He did not strike me when I spilt the tea."

"I was slow, but he didn't say anything."

"He said 'Thank you' when I brought him the blanket."

His kindness at first intrigued them, then drew them to him like moths; they could not stop whispering about him.

"He's already thirty but he's not married."

"I heard Grandmother say he won't marry till he has

passed some important examinations in China."

"I heard Grandmother say they have found a wife for him in China."

"Scholars like him don't want to marry."

"I don't want him to marry and go away to China. I want him to stay here and go on protecting me, as Ah Por would have done."

The words were never uttered, only deeply felt by Golden Frond, each time she crept into the circle of whispering bondmaids, but never leaving her own safe, reassuring circle of this man's presence. For the austere nobility of his scholar's mien and manner, like the gentle piety of Ah Por before him, had the power of repulsing the unruly forces in the house so that Golden Frond had stepped from one warm shelter into another, and could continue to feel safe. She hung around him, anticipating his every need. He hardly spoke to her but she knew every fibre of his body resonated to every distress signal from hers. Otherwise, how was she to explain his sudden appearance at the doorway to the kitchen, at precisely the moment when Older Cousin, importuning and slobbering, moved aside the braids of hair on her neck to kiss her? In the blistering scorn of his look, as he stood there in the doorway, tall and gaunt, Older Cousin had slunk away. Or his sudden loud call to her from his room downstairs (and he so seldom called to her) at the moment that Grandfather decided that the back-knocking should stop and swung round with menace?

She worshipped him; she was ready to die for him. The sounds of the men in the house awakening in the morning – the crackling expectorations of phlegm from throat, the steamy hissing of urine into chamber-pots – continued to galvanise bondmaids into feverish morning activity (a younger bondmaid, aged ten years old, had taken over the tasks from her), but the sound she listened to was the shuffling of papers and books on desk and a small cough which she had learnt to distinguish from other coughs. In a sly and determined way, she had edged a fellow bondmaid out of the duty of making his bed and sweeping his room, and taken this duty upon herself, giving it every loving attention.

Pig, who did not like her, complained secretly to Grandmother and told one or two more things besides.

"Golden Frond, it is not proper for you to go so often to Older Brother's room. You don't have to clean it so often."

"Yes, Grandmother," said Golden Frond and went on nevertheless. She thought of him as she lay awake at night, and turned over in her mind each of the words (never many) he had said to her during the day, detecting a new kindness here, a new depth of feeling there. Each of a man's words, let drop in tenderness to a woman, is never left there but picked up by her and turned over and cast this way and that, to catch at more meaning, and if there is none, will soon gather around itself the meanings supplied by the heart's yearning.

She sang a joyous song in the refuge of his protective power.

One day, while they were alone in the house (oh rare occasion!) he told her something. He said he was going away to China, and would be away for many months. He had this very important examination to take.

Her eyes filled with tears which she was helpless to stop, no matter how much she blinked, bit her lips, bit a corner of her handkerchief, and so she stood there, more miserable than at any time in her life. He was standing with his back to her, looking out of the window, upon a sea of old tiled roofs with desolate tufts of grass in the crevices and a flock of plaintive pigeons wheeling above. At the moment that he spun round upon hearing a small suppressed sob, she looked up at him, frightened and miserable, and when he walked to her, took her hand and led her to a chair, she knew the endurance had reached its end: she burst out in the full release of an overcharged heart. Her sobbing intensified with the gentle pressure of his hand upon her shoulder and the sound of his voice, barely audible, for he too was deeply moved: "Don't cry." How could she explain that a man's kindness to a woman, more than his cruelty, drew tears?

It turned out that though he was going to China, he was not going to take a wife. All those rumours about a wife waiting for him there were groundless and stupid, he said. She stared at him, hope breaking through the tear stains. The woman who in her imagination had tormented her for months, standing between them and blocking out their view of each other, was now vanquished. But what a hope! Worse than groundless, worse than stupid. She, a bondmaid of no parentage or name, the lowest of the low among women and he, a scholar of good family, destined for wealth and power.

In the moment of her banishing the hope forever, he rose to promise its fulfilment.

"I am going to make you my wife," he announced

with simple finality, "I shall make my wishes known to Grandmother who will see to arrangements for the required betrothal ceremony, and when I return from China, we shall be married."

He duly sought Grandmother's permission, dismissed the protestations, requested her to make the necessary arrangements and then continued quietly with his studies. Grandmother later said to her close friends, "What could I do? Men must have their way."

In the months that Older Brother was away in China, the sense of peace and well-being continued, for by virtue of the betrothal, his absence, as much as had his presence, encircled her with safety, while all round her were the ragings of appetite and doom. One night, the silence was broken by the screams of the bondmaid called 'Female' who had sat up suddenly upon the sleeping mat she shared with another bondmaid, and then staggered up and out of the room in a delirium. Grandmother, waking up in a fright, went to her, calmed her and then returned her to her mat. Mystery surrounded her whereabouts in the next few days, for she disappeared from the house the next day and was not seen again. She was brought home from the hospital on a stretcher and died the next morning. The story pieced together by the bondmaids, whispering urgently among themselves, was this: a few days before the delirious outburst, Female, in the fourth month of her pregnancy, had been quietly taken by Grandmother and a friend to a village abortionist, a Malay woman extremely skilled with her hands, but the abortion was a mess and Female developed complications. Grandmother tried to still the fever with home-made brews, but it continued unabated and Female was finally taken to hospital in a trishaw. She got worse and died after a few days, still screaming in her delirium.

"Ah Por, protect us all," prayed Golden Frond as she lit a joss-stick and stuck it in the urn on Ah Por's altar. She lit another joss-stick in gratitude for her special good fortune and yet another for the success of her betrothed in his examinations in China.

She was now eighteen years old; Grandfather was seventy-three; First Uncle was fifty-one and Older Cousin was twenty-six, and in the eleventh year of his imbecility.

She moved unafraid among them, strengthened by the love and kindness of a man. There were no letters from him because she could not read, but in the third month of his absence, she received, through a friend who had met up with him in China, the gift of a beautiful, red silk jacket. She would not even try on the jacket, but let it remain in its box, taking it out now and then to gaze upon the sheen of the silk and the fine embroidery of the peonies on the sleeves.

The news came with complete devastation. She was working on a beaded slipper, sewing on the eyes of a phoenix when she was told by Grandmother: Older Brother had died in China. He was midway through his examinations when he contracted a fever, got rapidly worse and died. She listened, then was aware of a numbness that locked up all powers of speech and movement so that only small, constricted sounds came from her throat and the eye-beads rolled away from her fingers, then of a penetrating chill and an enveloping darkness that sucked her into its centre making her gasp for breath.

She lay in a stupor for days. Grandmother called in the temple medium to say prayers and administer a drink that would ward off the final terrible bout of madness, for women, when the scorpions massed for the final onslaught, were known to try to escape it by hurling themselves out of windows or into wells.

She lay helpless on her bed, a pale and stricken ghost, making no sounds except the small groans of a misery too deep for tears. There were the dreams of her betrothed, alive and talking to her but these melted only too quickly into the dreams of him dead or in the throes of death, and there was always the dream, above all the tumult, of old Ah Por, benign and smiling and beckoning to her.

In this state, she heard voices around her, not the voices of people in dreams, but voices of real people, in Grandmother's room just next to hers.

"The temple medium says she must be given a husband, or she will die."

"Older Cousin needs a wife. He is already twenty-seven."

"She will be married to Older Cousin."

She began to pray to the Goddess Kuan Yin, to old Ah Por, to Older Brother, one after the other : "Protect me, save me", but it would appear that having given her protection and love for so long, they were now weary of her incessant calls and were leaving her to take care of herself.

She put her forehead to the floor in utmost supplication, but it seemed they had abandoned her to the darkness.

Older Cousin, grossly fat and leering, met her in the

corridor as she was getting out of her room for the first time since her illness, and shrieked in gloating triumph.

"You are to be my wife. The temple medium and Grandmother say so!"

"Not so," she said haughtily, though she could barely speak for weakness. "I must have a husband, but it will not be you."

"Oh! Oh!" The unwonted defiance robbed him of speech for a minute, and he gaped at her, his mouth opening and closing like a fish.

"Wait till I tell Grandmother!" he blurted.

"I do not care who you tell," she said with still greater hauteur, looking him all over with scorn. He danced around her in his rage and then ran off squeaking.

He ran off to complain to Grandmother and to demand that the bondmaid be whipped for her insolence, since she was well enough recovered from her illness. When the two of them went up to her room, they were in time to see the flames springing up and enclosing her body in a fiery embrace, as she sat, cross-legged, with hands prayerfully clasped in front of a hastily set up altar on which was a framed photograph of her betrothed. Grandmother shouted for help, Older Cousin began to jump up and down in the manner of an overwrought child unable to control his excitement. Blubbering, he pointed a trembling finger at the perfectly still figure in the flames, radiant in the red silk jacket. At the moment when somebody dragged in a mat and tried to beat out the flames, the figure keeled over in a graceful arc and lay face down, the song of immolation still on her lips.

VII

The Solace Of Guilt

In the Talmud and the Kabbalah are accounts of Lilith, the first wife of Adam. She had been made of the dust of the earth, as Adam had been made, and he was not pleased. He commanded her to lie beneath him, as a sign that she was inferior to him. But they said she refused to lie beneath him, insisting that the only love she would have was love with mutual respect. Angered by her pride, they began to deride her, and spread stories about her, insisting that she was the demon of the night, encouraging men to spill their sperm. She, the woman with strength, was transformed into a temptress of men.

*(From **TWBOS**)*

He was forty-seven years old, and he was about to take his first prostitute: she was coming up to his room, as arranged, in half an hour.

The thought amused him and brought on a slow ruminative smile. The amusement was not in the contemplation of an absurdly long postponement of a necessary rite of passage ("What? Never had one in your life? What sort of man are you?" Benny had said), or of the much-vaunted insecurity of the middle years, or even of the need of a virtuous man to take a break from virtue. Indeed, Andrew Chin was not sure why he was feeling so amused. Perhaps the word did not sufficiently describe the whole complex of pleasurable thoughts and sensations he was experiencing as he sat on the bed in the hotel room. Perhaps it was no more than the schoolboy's sense of self-gratification at a first prank about to be carried out.

"Bye! Be good!" his wife had said at the airport. The parting advice was more in the nature of the teasing raillery between husband and wife completely at ease with each other, than of any serious admonition to a departing spouse.

"Bye," he had said cheerfully, adding, "I should not be good in a place like Bangkok, no man's supposed to be good in Bangkok," echoing the irrepressible Benny who visited the city at least once a month and made no secret of it. His wife, laughing good-naturedly, kissed him and he was off.

And now the teasing words were about to become fact, for he was about to have his first prostitute. It had not been intended this way. He had planned, in the one day left after completing the business for his company, to explore the city's famed temples, markets and shops and pick up the obligatory Thai silk for his wife, gifts for his daughters and souvenirs for his secretary and the other girls at the office. The brochures at the hotel hinted of more exotic enjoyment, but these were not part of his world ("What!" Benny would have expostulated. "Go to Bangkok and not see these? What sort of tourist are you? Why, when I was there the last time, I went to the – Go, man. You won't believe until you see with your own eyes. My God! You know what the dancing girls do? They have these bottle caps, see – It's incredible, man –", finishing with his famous guffaw). So it was to be innocuous temples, markets and shops. But entering his room after lunch, he noticed a slip of pink paper under the door. He picked it up and read with increasing amusement: 'Virgin Prostitutes. Genuine. No Fake. With Good Proof in Certificate of Virgin, has signature of 2 doctor. If not satisfy, can refund.'

Andrew put the pink slip into his pocket, intending to take it home to show his wife who was an English Language teacher. But the little advertisement had a curious power which began to work on him, so that as he sat on his bed, he began to think strange thoughts which translated into strange sensations.

When he was a little boy of eight and staying with his grandparents, he hid himself one day behind the curtains when he heard his grandfather come in from the rain and speaking to a bondmaid who happened to be the only one in the house then, apart from himself. He knew for a certainty that his grandfather had never intended to go out at all, and would be back as soon as the others were out of the house. He also knew that his grandfather's curt order to the maid to take up a cup of hot tea to him in his room was no routine instruction.

Something was about to happen, and as soon as he heard the door softly closing after them, he darted out from behind the curtains, climbed the stairs noiselessly, then lay flat on his stomach outside the locked room to peep up through the convenient slit between door and floor. He watched, fascinated, and was later to connect the intense pleasure, approaching ecstasy, that he had seen on his grandfather's face, with the appropriation of virginity. A physiological intricacy beyond his little mind to grasp, he nevertheless understood its tremendous value through listening in on the many adult conversations in that large household of women. The knowledge, with the myriad trivia of childhood, had faded away as he grew up, but now in the tantalising pronouncements of the pink paper slipped under his door in the Bangkok hotel, it came back with vividness and power and insinuated itself into his very being, climaxing always with the recollection of pure ecstasy on his grandfather's face.

Andrew paced the room with the pink paper in his hand, his face mobile with a hundred flitting expressions. He was interested, awed, fascinated, alarmed at his own daring, and so curious about an experience at once commonplace and unique that no less than direct personal experience, he decided, could satisfy that curiosity. The realisation that he was forty-seven years old and with perhaps but a short time left for initiation into that experience, contributed to the decision. Having made up his mind, he was aware of a new lightness of being and of his whole body being suffused with a tingling glow of most delicious anticipation. He looked at the telephone number on the pink paper and realised that the simple act of his picking up the phone would be his induction into a totally new world. He wondered what he should say and how he should react if the pink paper people got crude or demanding, and as if to spare him all the hassle, a polite knock was heard on the door and a very polite-looking young man appeared and asked if he could be of any help.

So the girl was to come in precisely half an hour. And she was to spend the night with him.

Like the prankish schoolboy who longs for an audience, Andrew wondered, "What would Benny say?" He knew what Benny would say: the coarse, florid face with the raucous laugh loomed before his eyes, and made him shake his head and smile to himself. What would his wife say? The thought was totally irrelevant to and therefore had no place in this unique, tantalising, once-in-a-lifetime, just-for-the-experience adventure, which of course he had no intention of repeating.

There came a very timid knock, and the girl was admitted.

She was very young-looking, was probably no more than sixteen. She stood before him uncertainly, then took out a roll of paper from her pocket to give to him; it was the Virginity Certificate, attesting to her pristine state, signed by two doctors, one signature beside the other, in a corner of the gold-bordered scroll.

Andrew looked at her with increasing curiosity, then pleasure. A grotesquely made-up harridan with jangling ear-rings, low-cut skin-tight dress and stiletto heels and working the chewing gum endlessly in her cheeks (a portrait he derived exclusively from American TV) would have repulsed him. This girl who stood before him was young and pretty and innocent-looking, with a round face, large round eyes and a small mouth. Her abundance of dark curly hair was swept back and kept in place by a yellow head-band from under which a cluster of small tendrils escaped to frame her face in the most appealing way. She was wearing a frilly yellow dress which was one or two sizes too large, and high heels too high, so that she tottered a little as she walked up to him to show him the virginity certificate. He suddenly had a fleeting vision of her in another setting, her native village, divested of make-up, frilly dress and high heels, wearing the native sarong and walking barefoot with a water-pot on her head, a pink frangipani in her hair.

He gestured to her to sit down and she sat in the chair opposite him, balancing on the edge, in continuing deferential timidity. He began to speak to her slowly and gently, in English, asking simple questions. In response, she rattled off a string of rehearsed sentences in English, the only intelligible ones being "My name Porntip" and "I am virgin", the second followed by what sounded like a statement of a virgin's fee. They smiled continuously at each other and now and then laughed with shy amiability.

The sense of exhilaration on the approaching consummation of the ultimate frolic could not be resisted any longer and shedding whatever remaining tentativeness, Andrew got up, walked to Porntip and led her decisively to the bed. This was the cue, clearly, for her to initiate the process of disrobing: she pulled down the back zipper of her dress, stepped out of it and out of her high heels, in one movement of practised efficiency and ease. Then with the same sense of purpose, she lay down on the bed in her black lace bra and panties, watching him closely for the second cue as to who should be the one to effect the last stage of the disrobing, for a more enjoyable preliminary. He watched with mounting excitement and interest, all the while marvelling at the novelty of the experience. He was forty-seven and about to take his first prostitute, and so far everything had been exactly as he would have wished.

The girl looked at him, then decided to take the initiative, unclasping her bra, pulling down her panties and coming close to him in the full warmth of her naked beauties. He immediately pulled her down with a grunt of intense desire, rivalling even his grandfather's.

At the moment of the breaking, she gave the inevitable sharp cry, then when he had rolled off her and was quietly contemplating her from his easeful position on a mound of pillows, his arms behind his head, she pulled up from somewhere under her body the proof of the stained white cloth, and showed it to him, smiling. The crude contrivance, not just of the cloth, but of the practised sharp cry of pain, and of the forced orgiastic contortions of face and limbs irritated him. The irritation was not directed at the girl but at the whole set-up of parasites intent upon living off her, from the manager of the hotel to the young polite-looking pimp who had come to his door, to her parents who had probably already sold her, body and soul, to the hotel. The girl's total naturalness and simplicity left her untouched in any way by the sordid business so that whatever she did from obedience, no matter how crude, only enhanced her appeal.

He wanted to talk to her, to find out more about her, but her ability in the language had ended with the rattled off string of sentences and now, having been previously instructed to be with the man throughout the night, she settled compliantly by his side and watched for his every wish. His last thought, before he finally fell asleep, with the girl nestling against him, was of a very satisfactory first adventure and of the possibility that it need not be the last.

He woke up in the middle of the night with a start, thinking he was at home. Then he remembered and stretched out his hand to touch the girl beside him. He propped himself up on his elbow in alarm, for she was no longer there. He stretched out his hand quickly to feel for his watch and wallet on the beside table ("Never leave your watch or wallet or other valuables lying around in the room," Benny had cautioned, "And never accept any drink from a prostitute. It's sure to be spiked, and you'll wake up to find yourself stripped bare.") They were there, intact. Where could Porntip be? He had paid for a full night. She should not have left. He would have to complain to the manager.

He noticed the light in the bathroom and heard some very small sounds coming from it. Getting noiselessly out of bed, he padded across the room to peep through the imperfectly closed door.

Porntip was squatting on the bathroom floor, playing 'Five Stones'. She scattered five small pebbles on the floor in front of her, picked one up, threw it high into the air, scooped up the remaining four from the floor in one swift sweep, and was in time to catch the falling pebble, to complete the set of five in her little palm. She repeated the process, scattering the pebbles yet further apart, to challenge herself to higher levels of dexterity. With each success, she laughed softly to herself, with each failure, she frowned and muttered scolding words to the errant pebble that had not allowed itself to be scooped up in time with the others, or that had perversely slipped out between her fingers. With a child's total absorption at play, she did not see him watching her.

She was just that, a child. She was a child forced into an occupation that she understood only in terms of what she must do and say to please men and what she must not do and say to avoid the beatings from managers, pimps and parents. Her childhood had been stolen from her, but she stole back whatever bits of it she could, waiting till the men were asleep and snoring, to go into the bathroom, bring out her five stones and play by herself. While the men mauled her in bed, she pretended to smile and giggle and let out pleasing cries of pleasure, but all the time she was thinking about the five little pebbles hidden in the pocket of her dress.

A sickening sensation of the hideousness of it all condensed into a tight constriction of throat and stomach, and he leaned against the wall, to steady himself. He had paid for a child and taken her to bed. The child was probably no older than his younger daughter, Adeline, aged thirteen. He and his wife escorted Adeline to her school parties, forbade her to stay late and watched over her with greatest parental care and tenderness. If Porntip had been his daughter, she would have had the same loving protection. With his money he had made this child, working as a prostitute in a hotel, do unspeakable things for his pleasure, and she had complied fully, smiling, knowing that any complaint from him would mean the whip and lash. He had noticed a healed scar on her left thigh, probably the price she had paid for a flare of the child's rebelliousness that was never repeated.

She was singing a song softly to herself and he thought he understood the words.

Stones, pretty stones
Bright stones
Fingers, nimble fingers
But why did you have to open
Like legs?

He moved; he was not sure what he was going to do or say, except that an overpowering feeling of compassion for her and loathing for himself needed expression. The involuntary movement caused the child to look up with a start; she saw him and let out a loud gasp. The stones fell from her fingers and she stood up trembling, staring at him with the terror-stricken look of someone caught in a heinous act and for whom escape was impossible. He pushed open the door, said "Porntip" and she fell down on her knees and began to cry, rocking her small body to and fro in her terror. He tried to touch her, to say comforting words, but the child's panic had gathered into one obsessive thought, that here was another thing done wrong, for which punishment would be immediate and painful, so that all his efforts to calm and reassure by tone or touch were futile and washed uselessly over her. She became hysterical, speaking very rapidly in her own language, still on her knees and alternately holding out her hands pleadingly and wringing them.

"Oh, please, please –" cried Andrew, and then thinking to get her out of her hysteria more effectively, he said, in a sharp voice, "Now, now, no need for all this," at the same time firmly gripping her shoulders to pull her up from the absurd kneeling position. She screamed, and began struggling with him as with an adversary, finally breaking free and running out of the bathroom and out of the room, in choked sobbing.

"Oh my God," cried Andrew, pale with shock at this sudden turn of events. He sat down on the bed, breathing heavily, in a turbulence of emotions from which two, guilt and fear, detached themselves to shape into an overpowering certainty that this would not be the end of the adventure, that something was about to happen to him soon. The sense of dread overcame him, and he fell back on the bed, gasping.

He jumped up upon hearing loud shouts coming from the street below, and without understanding what they were all about, he knew they were in some way connected with him. He listened, horrified. The shouts grew; he could visualise a massing of people in the scene of the tragedy, whatever it was, in the light of the street lamps. He put on his shirt and his trousers and heard a soft polite knock on the door. It was the young polite-looking man again, and this time the man's smile was strained by the seriousness of the news he had come to give, and by his earnest desire that his valued guest should not be at all inconvenienced by it. The girl, Porntip, in a quite unaccountable fit of madness, had run to the hotel balcony and fallen over a ledge. Quite unaccountable, the young man emphasised, and smiling reassuringly at Andrew, repeated that he was not to worry about it at all, as these things happened. It was best that they kept quiet about it and went on as if nothing had happened. Andrew rushed past him through the open door and he said, "Sir, but –"

Andrew stood with the cluster of onlookers, but the body on the wet road was already covered with a piece of canvas, a small foot peeping out from it. He felt a tide of nausea rising, and returned quickly to the hotel to throw up in the bathroom. He saw the five stones still on the floor and he began to cry. The next day, he left for home.

"You what–" Benny was aghast. He repeated, "That's utterly crazy, Andrew, and I advise you not to do it." For Andrew had told him the whole story and confided to him his decision for reparation. Guilt needed reparation which was its only solace.

When he was a very small child, probably no more than five or six, he suffered enormous guilt over the death of a sister. He had nightmares of his little sister's ghost coming to haunt him; it did not help that one of the bondmaids who took care of him, a young spiteful woman, often told him the story of how he was responsible for the baby's death, embellishing her narration to frighten the little hypersensitive boy into a state of sheer terror. What had happened was that during the post-war years when he was a mere toddler, milk was scarce, and whatever milk could be obtained was first given to sons, then only to daughters, if there was any remaining. He being the only male child had first preference; while he grew sleek and chubby, his sister dwindled away and finally died from an illness brought on by malnutrition. He had a recurring dream in which he saw a pan of milk being heated on the stove, then poured into a bottle, then put in a bucket of water to cool. His little sister cried for the milk but each time she tried to reach it, she was slapped down and finally pulled away. He saw himself drinking from the bottle of milk and being carried in a bondmaid's arms, and urging the bondmaid to take him to the window to look out upon the yard outside where he was sure his sister had been taken. Still drinking his milk, he looked out and saw her dead on the hard earth of the yard, like an enormous insect on its back, her arms and legs stiffly sticking out.

When he was older, he found out that there was a way by which the living could feed the dead and thus make atonement: every year, during the Feast of the Hungry Ghosts, people went to the graves of their relatives and laid out enormous feasts of food and drink.

His grandmother, taking him with her on her rounds of the graves, was surprised to see something drop out of his shirt and fall clanking to the ground where it hit a stone. It was a tin of condensed milk.

"Why, little grandson!" she had laughed. "Whatever have you got there?" He did not tell her, but it was an offering of propitiation to the dead sister who had died because of him.

The frightening dream disappeared. The ghost must have drunk the milk and forgiven him.

There was to be more guilt and more need of the solace of expiation.

His mother employed a servant, a remote relative who had a little adopted daughter. The child must have been about eight then, but was very small for her years, looking no more than five or six, and he was twelve. The Clever Scholar, the women in the household called him as they looked at him with pride, and all their energies were put to the service of his comfort and pleasure, he being the sole male child. Their attentiveness embarrassed him; their readiness to punish the servant's child on his account embarrassed him even more. Thus if the child followed him around in hopes of being given some of the bread-and-jam he was eating, or stood and watched him while he was doing his school homework and he frowned for her to go away, her mother would appear in a noisy display of the deference expected of the poor relative, shrilly scolding the child or slapping her till she cried. Between his genuine pity for this unfortunate little girl who was always sickly and never without scabs on her spindly legs, and his utter revulsion at her idiotic adulation of him, he grew irritable and difficult, often locking himself in his room for hours. One day he lost a favourite colouring pen, and was certain that the girl had taken it because he had seen her looking at it with intense interest. He asked her sternly, if she had taken his pen; the child blubbered, and immediately the incident was taken to a high level of adult antagonisms, his mother making insinuating remarks and the relative responding by beating the child in a frenzy of transferred hate. The child began to vomit and the distressed relative would still go on with the beating, until his mother coldly went up and removed the piece of firewood from her hand. He had meanwhile found the missing colouring pen; he had put it away in a drawer and had forgotten about it. Lacking the courage to tell the truth, he brooded in his room for days. The child was taken ill, and he remembered that his guilt was so keen that he emptied his money-box of its coins and went out to buy an enormous packet of biscuits which he hurriedly left beside the mattress on which the sick child was lying. He never saw her again and was told that she had died in hospital.

He did not tell Benny of these two childhood incidents, but he said, running his fingers through his hair in his deep distress, "You know three females have died on my account, and they were all children. I have been responsible for the deaths of three innocent children. How can I forgive myself?" Ignoring the histrionics, Benny said, "But Andrew, listen. You can't go to the family and offer money. They would fleece you dry. I know their kind; you would be a heaven-sent opportunity to them." For Andrew had told him of his secret intention to return to Bangkok and get the help of the hotel manager to locate the girl's family. He would then visit them and offer to pay for the funeral expenses and for whatever else was needed.

"That's the least I can do," said Andrew sorrowfully. The incident had changed him drastically. His wife wondered and agonised about this sudden change in her husband – his hair was greyer and he had aged overnight – but he would not tell her.

"Listen," said Benny again, with greater urgency in his voice. He worried about Andrew being mercilessly exploited by 'those people' and tried to dissuade him with all the horror stories he could muster: the American engineer who befriended a Thai bar waitress, sent her money faithfully for three years, only to be dumped by her; an Englishman who was cleaned out by his Thai wife and her family; a Singaporean businessman who returned from a trip totally disoriented and was later found to have been the victim of a magic potion administered by his Thai mistress.

"Don't," pleaded Benny, and this time there was exasperation in his voice: here was a guy making a big to-do over nothing and possibly ruining it for the other guys.

"Planeloads of Japanese go there every day," he said, still trying hard to dissuade Andrew from a patently futile mission, "and planeloads of French too. You only have to read the newspapers to know. It happens everywhere in the world. Do you mean to tell me," he said, "that each and every one of us should come home weeping with guilt and sorrow?"

It was with great difficulty and a considerable sum of money that Andrew managed to persuade the polite young man at the hotel to take him to see Porntip's family. He looked around at the squalor of the huts clustered on the muddy banks of a river; they seemed to be constructed of the same foetid substance as the debris washed up by the river. A group of small children with large, round bellies, matted hair and dirty faces gathered round him, giggling, and he began to dispense coins from his pocket. The group rapidly swelled into a crowd, and the children, jostling with each other, and tugging at his hands, shirt and trousers, clamoured for more. The young man shooed them off with both hands and led Andrew hurriedly to a small, ramshackle hut some distance from the river. Porntip had no father; he had died in an accident in a stone quarry a year back. Porntip's mother, a thin, dried woman with a grief-pinched face pointed to a table on which stood a picture of Porntip, smiling, with a frangipani in her hair, side by side with a picture of the dead father, and in front of the portraits, a saucer with flower petals and a lit candle. Porntip's mother began to weep; the tragedy of her life condensed into a long, thin wail as she sat beside the pictures of her husband and daughter and began beating on her chest. Pale with shock, Andrew drew out from his pocket some money, handed it to the young man beside him and requested him to explain to the woman that he would be grateful to be allowed to help out in the funeral and other expenses. The woman looked up sharply, looked from one face to the other and stared at the wad of money which represented remission from years of back-breaking work at the quarry; her cluster of children, similarly attracted, gathered round her to watch silently.

"It's the least I can do," said Andrew gently, and the young man translated. Andrew's eyes wandered and rested, with horror, on a young girl by the side of the hut, visible from the doorway, squatting on the hard earth, playing Five Stones. It was the same round face, the same abundance of hair, the same dexterity of hand in the sweeping up of the four pebbles to catch the falling fifth. Andrew stared, and a strangled sound came from his throat, as he raised a finger to point at her. The mother, following his finger, raised her voice and called shrilly. The name sounded like "Porntip." The girl heard, looked up, gathered her five stones and came in. She stood shyly before Andrew. The mother, smiling through her tears, introduced her. Her name was Wantip, and she was Porntip's younger sister. She smiled shyly and looked on the ground. The mother said something to the young man and he translated: "She says that you are a good and generous man. You can have Wantip. She is a virgin and will be a very good woman to you. She says she knows you will treat Wantip very well. She says –"

"No, you don't understand," blurted Andrew. The woman who understood very well, again said something to the young man who translated: "She says another man has already come to ask for her, and if you don't take her now –"

Wantip, on cue, walked up to Andrew, and stood before him, head bowed, hands reverentially clasped, then looked up at him with that mixture of pleading and promise in her large eyes and soft mouth.

VIII

The Revenge

Various are the legends of how Attis, the son-lover of the great goddess Cybele of Anatolia, met his death. The most appealing is the one that tells how one day as the young Attis was looking after his grazing sheep and playing his flute, unknown to him, the monster Agdistus was watching his youthful beauty with lustful eyes. Unable to control his passion any longer, Agdistus tried to force himself upon Attis. Utterly revolted, the pure Attis tore the genitals from his own body, bleeding to death under a tree rather than be unfaithful to his great goddess mother. The goddess on seeing the lifeless, emasculated body of her son-lover wept with sorrow. Picking him up gently from the ground that had sprung a thousand violets where the blood had spilt, she carried him, wrapped in woollen mourning bands to the mountain cave where she lived. She also took with her the tree under which he had died, planting it at the entrance to the cave and burying the body in the earth beneath. Every year, sitting under this tree on the anniversary of his death, she mourned for him, this faithful, loyal, devoted lover of hers who would rather deprive himself of his maleness than betray her.

(From ***TWBOS****)*

The daughter came home from the date tearful, and the mother guessed what had happened.

"He's not going to marry you after all, right?" she allowed herself some malice through the maternal concern. "Am I right or not?" And when the daughter set up a howl of desolation, she knew she was right.

"I told you so! I told you a hundred times that as soon as he had his way with you, he would dump you. They're all like that!" – remembering the time when her own husband would have dumped her once the disgrace of her growing belly was discovered, except that, upon the secret administration of the temple medium's magic potion in his drink, he suddenly turned docile and married her.

"How many times did he have his way with you?" she asked sharply.

The girl said, "Four."

The mother shook her head in exasperation. "I told you, didn't I, to be careful. A girl's gift is not for foolish squandering, and now you've spent it on a brute of a man who then leaves you, smacking his lips in search of others! You young women will never learn."

Her daughter wept noisily, unable to bear the loss of the young man and the folly of a squandered gift.

"Will you be seeing him again?" asked the mother after a while, and the daughter, hearing purpose in her voice, looked up and asked, "No – but why do you ask?"

"Because," said the mother, "you will need to put something in his drink."

It was a small packet of very fine ash, sifted from the remains of a prayer paper burnt together with a piece of the napkin that had touched the most secret part of the daughter's body.

The magic did not work. On the contrary, it hardened the young man's resolution not to marry the girl, but not before he had had his way with her again, making it the fifth time.

The daughter was disconsolate, and the mother furious. She paced the house at night, as restless as a caged animal. She had to take revenge on behalf of her daughter. Since the magic did not work, she would have to move to the next weapon in her arsenal. It was going to be extremely difficult, but she would know no peace till it had been accomplished.

Mother and daughter got together to work out the plan carefully, the daughter by now galvanised to an irrevocable fury and pitch of bloodthirstiness. The plan was in five steps: Step 1, invite him to dinner, lulling any suspicion with a show of genuine friendship and desire to forget the past; Step 2, he comes for dinner, feed him with his favourite food; Step 3, ply him with his favourite drink, but in a way as not to arouse any suspicion; Step 4, he feels sleepy, invite him to sleep on his favourite sofa in the sitting room, promising to wake him up soon; Step 5, he is snoring in his sleep, strike.

Everything went according to plan, until Step 5, when instead of snoring, he seemed to be sleeping fitfully, crossing and uncrossing his legs, and tossing about. However, after a while, the full effect of the drink was felt, and he began to be still and to snore loudly, his mouth wide open, one arm dangling at the side.

"Just a few minutes more, we need to be sure," said

the mother, and the daughter stood by, on the ready, her blood up. The mother held the knife, sharp, shining and deadly, in her hand.

"Ready," said the mother and the daughter carefully prised his legs apart, deftly unzipped his fly and brought out the offending member, now limp and helpless in her hand.

"You wronged me five times," she addressed it severely, as if it had a life of its own – and indeed, during those times, it seemed it did, rearing and moving its head like some predatory animal. "Here," said the mother, handing over the knife, and in simultaneous explosions of blood, screams of pain and shrieks of triumph, the target object was cut off and held aloft, between thumb and finger, a little nondescript trophy. The young man jumped up, screamed and screamed even more when he saw himself thus denuded. Covering the spot with both hands, his body bent double over it, he hopped about, wailing, not unlike the cartoon character or the comic hero of film and TV slapstick, who has just been kicked in the groin by the little lady, except that in this case, the groin was just not kicked, but killed, with the blood-spattered hands to prove it.

"Police! Call the police!" screamed the man, while the two women ran away, still carrying their prize. Outside in the darkness, they stopped near a drain that was sometimes half-filled with water, and threw the pathetic little piece in it, gurgling with demonic glee at the successful completion of their revenge.

"In Thailand," said the mother, "they feed it to the

ducks. I wish there were a duck or chicken just now." Then the women returned to the house and gave themselves up.

The manhood was lost forever, for after looking for it in the drain for almost an hour using powerful torches, the police called off the search and assumed that it had been washed away or eaten up by a fish or frog. The frantic young man, who had had hopes of it being found and reattached, settled into a state of permanent despair.

The women were unrepentant, and when asked why they did it, said they had to, giving the impression they would do it again.

The newspapers in Singapore were full of the story for days. It brought letters of sympathy which were equally bestowed upon the wronged women and the equally wronged man, but when there appeared a picture of the man, looking very depressed and saying that it was a fate worse than death, the sympathy shifted in his favour. Then somebody wrote in to ask the intriguing question: why did the women choose a form of revenge that invariably led to their being caught? The letter provoked a flurry of replies which examined the causes from a variety of angles – psychological, cultural, biological, political – from the need to turn penis envy into real action, to the instinct to preserve fellow women from the same sad fate, to the pure joy of proclaiming woman's only area of monopoly of power, since men could never retaliate ***in kind***.

Wrote a very upset male, "It boggles the mind to think what women are capable of doing; they can claim the superlatives of violent revenge!", followed by another, equally anguished: "Men, be forewarned. It may be necessary for us all to go around wearing groin guards!"

Both the women of course went to jail, the mother getting three years and the daughter five, and the last thing heard about the poor dispossessed young man was that he was seeking help from a witch doctor somewhere in a mountain village in Thailand.

IX

The Feast Of The Hungry Ghosts

... now consider the paucity of language in this respect. 'Purest', 'Fairest', Wisest', 'Bravest', 'Gentlest'. This is about all we can manage. How can the mere addition of three pitiful little letters 'e-s-t' hope to capture the full depth and width and breadth of the excellence that is Woman? Until we devise an adequate linguistic system for this purpose, we would have to be satisfied with the so-called superlatives in the language.

(From ***TWBOS****)*

A visitor would be struck by the grandeur of the building and even more by the grandeur of its purpose: to house the remains of one woman who had died more than fifty years ago. It was an immense structure with the inescapable curving pagoda roof to remind the Chinese emigrant of home, and to allow the gratification, since Filipino law did not permit him to own land, of owning great houses. When the house was ready to receive his dead wife, he must have further gloated, as he supervised the ceremony of transferring the remains to its new and permanent home, on the contrast between this house and the surrounding hovels of the natives. Indeed, the contrast would strike the visitor as positively obscene: the fully air-conditioned building with its tiled floors and marble pillars for one dead woman, and the tin-and-cardboard shacks clinging to the sides of denuded hills, home to hundreds of ragged women and children who regularly emerged to scrabble in the rubbish dumps close by.

But the real obscenity of contrast lay in the food: for the dead woman, one Madam Teh Siew Po, the altar table creaked with an abundance of roast pig, young white fowl steamed in their own pristine juices, the most finely spun rice noodles, herbal soups, pink sugared buns, peanut sweets, almond paste puddings, rare fungi, and even rarer sea cucumber cooked with fragrant cabbage, oranges, lichees, pomelos whose thick, soft skin was carved into a ring of delicately curving petals to reveal the succulent pink fruit inside, and for the living woman, one Mrs. Raphaela Santos and her family of seven children, ages ten to one, fistfuls of rice, boiled vegetables that had been salvaged from the rubbish dump and one fried fish which they were all to share.

This was the time of the annual Chinese Feast of the Hungry Ghosts, when Heaven and Hell emptied themselves of the spirits of the dead to allow them to return to Earth to be fed by their relatives in a continuing show of remembrance and love. No ghost was better fed than Madam Teh Siew Po; every year, since her death in 1936, the ghost feast had been held for her (even during the war years) and each year she came and partook of the magnificent spread. That she had actually returned could be ascertained by the simple procedure of leaving a tray of ash overnight on the altar table and checking it the next day for footprints (very small, for Madam Teh had bound feet). The caretaker, once he was assured of the fact, was free to dispose of the food as he liked. Over the years, the practice of packing the food in separate parcels to be distributed among various relatives had become a hassle for the old man, and lately, he had simply dumped the food outside the house and closed the gates again, in the full knowledge that within minutes, it would be grabbed up by the beggar woman with the seven children.

For three years running, Raphaela Santos and her brood had whooped with joy at the sight of the ghost food; in a highly efficient division of labour, they had, within minutes, packed up the good stuff in their paper bags, cardboard boxes, tin buckets and plastic mugs, and were carrying it home in triumph for a succession of family feasts. By gathering up the unfinished remnants and boiling them in a rich stew, Raphaela Santos was actually able to extend the annual celebration by a few more days.

Then disaster struck. That year, no footprints were seen in the ash, therefore the ghost had not come, therefore the food could not be removed. Raphaela waited in great anxiety, straining her neck to peep through the window. She saw the splendid offerings on the altar table, the centrepiece being always the roast pig, in their porcelain dishes and tureens, amidst flickering candles, joss-sticks and flowers, and the old caretaker snoozing in his folding chair nearby. She saw him get up and go to examine the tray of ash, and held her breath, as he closely turned the tray this way and that in the sunlight, to catch any imprint. No, there was none, and he put back the tray and returned to his chair.

Raphaela fretted fearfully; if Madam Teh did not appear soon, the food would surely spoil. The weather was hotter than usual, and the air conditioning would be no guarantee.

On the fourth day, the caretaker, squinting at the ash and detecting a faint print near the centre of the tray, decided that the ghost had at last appeared. But it was too late! With a heart near to breaking, Raphaela and her seven children, her newest baby on her hip, watched the caretaker empty each plate and tureen into large black plastic bags, tie up the bags securely, then carry them to dump into the refuse bins outside. They waited for him to get back into the house, then closed in, making frantic little noises as they untied each bag to see what could be saved. It was no use; all the food had gone quite bad.

The next year, as the Feast approached once more, the hopes rose again. The eternal roast pig, roasted to precisely that point when the crispy, crunchy skin detached itself to provide a separate, purer eating pleasure, the shiny white steamed chickens carried in a bunch by their necks, the mountain of pink, sugared buns shaped like peaches and women's breasts – Raphaela's children could describe each item in perfection of detail, as it was carried into the house by the caterer. She said to them, "Hush, we'll wait and see; we don't know what will happen," remembering the bitterness of the previous year's experience.

They waited, with held breath, their eyes never leaving the Great House, so that they could be the first to run up and lay claim to the booty. The waiting seemed interminable, and Raphaela, knowing that their next meal would be from ghosts or never, began to fret and mutter her fears out loud.

"The weather's much hotter this year. The soup will be the first to go, and then the vegetables. The roast pig may be saved yet."

She continued sullenly, "Some people who have all the food they want, even when they are dead, have no thought for others who go hungry all the time."

She prayed to the saint whose name she bore, and whose holy image she wore in a small brass medal on a string round her neck: 'O holy St Raphael, Helper of the Innocents and the Suffering, help me!'

The afternoon sun continued to beat down pitilessly; Raphaela's head began to spin giddily and when it cleared, she saw, not the angel but Madam Teh Siew Po, exactly as she had appeared in the photograph on the altar table: a plain, almost sad face, the severe hairstyle of the time not detracting from the youthfulness of the features. She was sitting, as in the photograph, in an ornate high-backed chair, small and slim-looking despite the loose, long-sleeved black silk blouse and baggy black silk trousers, her bejewelled fingers stiffly spread out on her knees, her tiny feet in pointed, embroidered shoes.

Raphaela stared; she noted the perfect plucked arches over the large sad eyes, the tiny lucky mole above the right upper lip. Half a century separated the two women, and more than half of Fate's injustice, for one received only eggs and the other only scorpions: the wealthy and protected Chinese woman who never knew a day of want in life or death, and the Filipino slum woman, abandoned by her husband and lover, with seven children to support and herself to die soon from a suppurating stomach wound because she did not have the money to pay for an operation. But just now, the concern was more immediate, for food in the stomach, and Raphaela Santos, with all the energy she could muster, spoke to Madam Teh Siew Po across the immense gulfs.

"I have been waiting for so long. Will you please come, or it will be too late! It will spoil!"

She repeated, with mounting exasperation, "Please come. We have not eaten for two days!" The sad, child-like face looked back at her; Raphaela saw, with surprise, the intense friendly interest that was suddenly irradiating the plain features, and felt ashamed of her own ungraciousness.

"I didn't mean to be rude," she said, "I was just so very hungry and desperate that I sounded rude but then –," with sudden shrewdness, "we are sisters, are we not, and sisters can bare their sad hearts to each other, can they not?"

The irradiated face nodded assent and Raphaela, beginning to feel once more the oppression of the afternoon heat, shook her head vigorously, rubbed her eyes, and opened them to see the face gone and at her feet, a rabbit, sitting up, ears twitching.

"My, my!" she cried. "A rabbit. Enough food for the whole family." She was sure it was sent by that strange Chinese woman whom she had just spoken to; no rabbit would ever be found in the vicinity, as any four-footed population would have long ago been decimated by the slum children.

"Come, rabbit dinner!" she said, struck by the whimsicality of the dead woman. But the creature darted away, in the direction of the Great House and was lost to sight. "Rabbit dinner gone," she said, shrugging her shoulders and playing up to the whimsicality but at the same time thinking it rather unkind of the Chinese woman to play a trick like that on her. She was going to make her sad, hungry way home when she heard the caretaker calling her and beckoning to her.

"She's come," he said matter-of-factly, "so you can have the food. You're lucky it's still good." She saw the basis of his confident announcement – four deep, certainly unmistakable, prints in the ash, very small, like a woman's bound feet, but also very, very like a rabbit's paw prints. She wanted to ask the caretaker, "Did you see a rabbit come in just now?" but decided in a sudden access of new found joy that it ought to remain a secret, a secret of loving sisters who could reach out to each other in remembrance and compassion across great gulfs of time.

X

Transit To Heaven

In the sacred texts of the Vedas, it is said: where women are worshipped, the Gods will be pleased.

(From ***TWBOS****)*

In the very short time (a few seconds of earth time?) before her soul detached from her body and started drifting away, her entire life was presented to her eyes. It is true then, thought Dora Warren, Feminist Extraordinaire, what they say about the drowning man in the last moments before he goes under, or the leaping woman just before she hits the pavement: their life appears before them in a sweep of intense colour and emotion. She had read of the thrilling chronological rainbow – arc of life's passages, from childhood through adolescence to the mature and mellowing years, that made the departing soul suddenly ache to come back to reclaim lost loves, but in her case, there was none of this longing, only an impatience to have this presentation, clearly a rite of passage, over and done with quickly, so that she could move on. She was excited about the prospect of arriving at her destination.

Meanwhile, the obligatory review.

It came in clear, separate, hard-edged pictures, one after the other – click, click – like slides projected on to a screen by a slide-projector. The first one showed her as a little, pig-tailed girl being coaxed away from her mother's side by a visitor anxious to have her play with a small belligerent-looking boy carrying a blue plastic gun. She saw that while the visitor beamed indulgently as the gun-toting boy dragged her out to play in the garden, her mother looked a little nervous and once or twice craned her neck to look out and ascertain that all was well. Five minutes later, her mother and the visitor came running out of the house upon hearing a piercing scream, her mother exclaiming, "Oh, my poor little Dorrie, are you all right?" and the visitor saying reassuringly, "It's okay, Marge. Chuck only frightens a little, he means no harm", before they pulled themselves up in front of the kennel at the bottom of the garden where the screams were coming from, and let out a joint gasp: for cowering inside the kennel was the boy, mere jelly in his terror, and standing guard over him with the gun pointed between his eyes, was Dora Warren, aged five, her pigtails flying.

Dora chuckled.

Despite the incident, she had gone on to marry Charles at age nineteen, mesmerised by his good looks, his enormous biceps, his towering strength.

Click. Dora now watched, fascinated, as the baby was slowly pulled out of her, raw and bloody and slimy, its small face twisted in the rictus of birth.

"How beautiful! How simply beautiful!" cried the exhausted mother on the hospital bed, but the father who had insisted on witnessing the birth turned pale, gasped, swooned and fell upon the floor, hitting his head with a loud thud. Attention had to be temporarily diverted from the squalling new-born baby to its father knocked out cold on the floor while Dora, raising herself to look, cried out anxiously, "Honey, are you okay?"

That was probably the turning point in her life. In an apocalyptic flash, she saw what she had only vaguely suspected all along: that man was much weaker than woman. Thundering, marauding, weapon-wielding man was far weaker than procreating, nurturing woman with her baby at her breast.

Strip a man of his carapace and you saw a soft quivering core of fears inside; the grown man fainting at the sight of the woman giving birth, and the small boy throwing away his weapon in terror of the little girl and hiding in the kennel, were one and the same. To hide their fears they developed all sorts of myths and theories such as that of the treacherous Eve and of Penis Envy, to confuse and intimidate women into a state of subjugation.

The discovery was exhilarating, but it would be years before she would develop it into a counter theory to present to the world in a dramatic exposé of the male sex.

The celestial slide-projector cooperatively skipped those humiliating years of fights and tears and the final divorce to concentrate on the greatest triumph in her life. "Runaway Bestseller by First-time Feminist Writer: Penis Envy and Pronoun Envy? Phooey to the Greatest Phallacy ever Told!" accompanied by a picture of her at the launching of her book, beamingly autographing the five thousandth copy. It had been a thoroughly researched book for which she had actually made an extensive trip to the Far East, having heard of mysterious customs of women bowing and offering gifts to gods with incredibly large priapuses, whether fashioned out of wood, stone or rice dough. Everywhere she went, she saw evidence of this worship – gifts of boiled rice, fruit and flowers in temples, shrines, caves, houses, the roadside – and happily took pictures and made notes. She was stunned by the pervasiveness of the belief but buoyant at the prospect of singlehandedly destroying it, and so save fellow women at last from the worst form of enslavement by men. So the Far East trip which took her through India, Japan, the Philippines, Thailand and Indonesia was thoroughly enjoyable, except for one small, frightening incident in India, which, however, she soon dismissed from her mind.

She was alone at a railway station in Allahabad late at night and was walking along a wooden platform in the dim orange light when she became aware of large bundles of rags strewn along the side. As she watched, curious, one stirred, opened, and a face appeared, that of a young woman, skeletal in its deep hollows, and then another, that of a small child with large, unmoving eyes. The woman crawled out of the bundle of rags towards her, carrying the child in one arm and stretching out the other to her, in an infinity of pleading, and she saw, to her further horror, that the arm was a mere stump, hacked at the elbow. The woman crawled closer, looked up at her and smiled, her arm stretched out in an enormous effort to touch her. Recoiling in terror, Dora opened her bag, pulled out a sheaf of money, flung it down upon the ground between herself and the woman, and fled, turning round just once, to see the woman still crawling towards her and past the money, arm still stretched out for the touch of sisterliness. Dora fled into the darkness and very soon left the country, and the incident was forgotten back home in the whirl of excitement that attended the publication of her sensational book.

Dora chuckled as she saw herself borne aloft in a churning sea of women, her long blonde hair shaved off in a gesture of defiance, and beside her, fluttering in the evening breeze, the banner proclaiming "The Bald Truth about Man's Oppression of Woman." She stopped chuckling, stared and said, "Oh my Josie, my poor little Josie," for she had noticed a small, five-year-old girl in a red coat, standing forlornly in the crowd, clutching a rag doll.

"Mother! Mother!" the child screamed, but the screams were drowned in the wild hurrahs.

Thoroughly intoxicated by her success, she had gone on to produce a giddy string of equally successful books: *Woman: The Foundation Of Society That Should Not Have Got Laid*, *Herstory Of The World, In Definitely More Than 10 1/2 Chapters*, *Adam And Even*, the last carrying the definitive message that the time for redress was now or never.

Click. Click. Click.

Dora Warren. Dora Warren. Dora Warren.

She had become a household name.

You are our voice.

You have saved us.

From now onwards, women's issues can only be meaningfully discussed in terms of two categories, B.D.W.

and A.D.W. – Before Dora Warren and After Dora Warren.

Dora, thank you.

Thank you for daring to be the lone voice in the wilderness.

The familiar face on TV, with the wide eyes and Wife of Bath gap-tooth raised cheers.

She loved the adulation.

And then things began to go wrong, terribly wrong. She was inclined to put the blame on Josie.

"My mother's the most bizarre person I have ever met," said the self-assured young lady in an interview in her college during the long period when Dora went into seclusion in the Mexican desert to reflect and work on the final grand theory about man's victimisation of woman. The newspaper proclaimed with glee the next day: "'My Mother's the Most Bizarre Person I have Ever Met', says Feminist Dora Warren's Daughter."

In the quiet of the desert, she meditated and worked and had her second apocalyptic flash: man's most enduring weapon against woman was not the phallus, as she had previously believed, but language. Man had been using language to enslave woman for hundreds of years and he did it with such cunning that woman suspected nothing and fell into his trap, so that each time she opened her mouth to speak, she fell deeper. Man's privileging of language, the most precious human heritage, was his most successful ploy to hide his weakness and perpetuate the myth of his strength.

Awe-struck by the ingenuity of her own intellectual processes that had led to the unlocking of this secret,

Dora Warren was soon galvanised into feverish activity to make it known to the world. She searched the language for proof and came up with armfuls which she triumphantly flung at her stunned audiences.

"Listen carefully," she thundered. "While words like 'master', 'lord', 'bachelor' and 'wizard' have acquired new meanings of approval and admiration, the exact opposite has happened to their feminine equivalents. 'Mistress', 'madam', 'spinster' and 'witch' have been degraded to the point that we are immediately condemned by their application. Oh, the negative associations that have accreted around words used by men to shame woman! Do you not recoil at 'Black Maria'? Why does a maximum-security vehicle for hard-core criminals have to bear a woman's name? Are you not revolted by 'Venus Trap'? Why does a killer jungle flower, a total botanical aberration, have to be named after a woman? Men want to subjugate us by making us cringe in shame! And they have succeeded! Sisters, we must get out of this Shame Syndrome!"

Dora Warren's eyes swept over the audience in a blaze of fury.

"Listen to this," she boomed with growing menace. "'Arabella Destroys 10,000 Homes.' 'Death Toll from Lizzie's Fury Reaches 6,000.' 'Amanda Screams Across California: More Damage Expected.' Why do men name hurricanes and tornadoes and typhoons and the most destructive of nature's forces after women? Why, to make us feel guilty and cow us further. Sisters, let's rid ourselves of this Guilt Syndrome!"

Dora Warren stood to her full height in the glare of the

TV lights, put one fist on her hip and with the other, began to punch the air.

"Are you aware," she shrieked, "that the language is riddled with words that condemn us to a class of beings with no identity of our own, so that we can only define ourselves in relation to men? Manageresses and authoresses and poetesses and waitresses are nothing more than little appendages of 'esses', totally dependent on males for their existence! Sisters, this dependency is not just the result of specific terms in the language but of its very structure and grammar! You know what I did?" And since the audience did not know what she did, she told them.

"I went round with a little secret tape-recorder in my handbag and taped one hundred conversations of men and women," she announced with aplomb. "And do you know what shocking discoveries I made?" The audience gazed at her spellbound.

"I discovered," bellowed Dora Warren, "that women use the Question Tag eighty-two percent more than men! Do you know what it means when a woman continually says to a man, 'It's going to rain, isn't it?' 'I'm not too late, am I?' 'You will pick me up at eight, won't you?' It means that she is continually seeking confirmation, validation, assurance and approval from a man. She is saying her own judgment and feelings are suspended until a man endorses them! She is nothing without him, a nonentity, a nought, a cipher, a no-thing. She is a dependency class that lives on the surplus of man's approval, like the first foolish woman born out of a man's redundant rib! Let us get out of this Redundancy Syndrome!"

On a rampage of talks, seminars and workshops through the country, Dora Warren urged women to pull themselves out of the Shame, Guilt, and Redundancy Syndromes. She organized demonstrations to heckle recalcitrant sisters who still allowed themselves to be addressed as 'chairman' or to be called 'waitress.'

At this stage, some confusion set in. While the women had been totally in agreement with the need to get rid of the Phallacy Syndrome and indeed had participated most enthusiastically in the demonstrations of protest during which objects conspicuously cylindrical in shape or projectile in function were symbolically set ablaze in a tremendous bonfire, they were less sure about the other syndromes which seemed more abstract and therefore less comprehensible. Already some women were beginning to ask each other: "What's happening to Dora Warren? What's she talking about? Can we continue to trust her?"

"Tell us, Dora Warren," one of them asked boldly, "how come if women are so oppressed by men, they live longer? The statistics show that worldwide, women outlive men by an average of five years."

"True!" cried Dora. "But what's the use of living longer to suffer more? It just means five more years of oppression, that's all. Would you like to be that woman who, when she was about to draw her last breath, instructed that her epitaph should be these words: 'She died at thirty, and was buried at sixty'?" She looked round challengingly.

"I read in an article somewhere," said another woman in the audience, "that in a survey conducted among women to find out how many of them would like to be reborn as men in their next life, eighty-one per cent said 'No', they would prefer to be reborn as women. Now how would you account for that?"

"Ah, this proves my point!" cried Dora. "It shows how very much oppressed women are, for they want to come back to take revenge on their oppressors, and nobody avenges like a woman!"

The heckler sat down, nonplussed. But the confusion and disillusionment had set in, and that was the beginning of Dora Warren's fall.

One night, Dora looked up at the bright stars, breathed deeply, reflected and was struck by another blinding flash on her road to the Damascus of woman's liberation from man. The discovery was so electrifying that she had to sit down for a while and steady herself. Then she got up, stretched her arms out to the stars and exclaimed, "This is going to be the apotheosis of my career! The grand theory at last! My magnum opus!"

She announced to the world that she had discovered the three most insidious words in the language, whose excision would free woman, once and for all. The audience held their breath, as Dora Warren gathered hers to deliver the ultimate coup de grâce.

"I love you!" she screeched to the audience. "The three most sinister words in the language are 'I love you'. Men have been enslaving women for thousands of years with these words, and women, in responding, have put the seal of acceptance on their own doom. In the Japanese language," continued Dora, her eyes taking in the entire audience in one imperious sweep, "there is a little suffix 'yo' sometimes used at the end of an utterance. It has different meanings for men and women. When a man says, 'Jack and Jill went up the hill, yo,' he means, 'Jack and Jill went up the hill, I'm telling you this and you had better believe it!' but when a woman says, 'Jack and Jill went up the hill, yo,' she means 'Jack and Jill went up the hill, and will you be so kind as to believe me.' Now," went on Dora Warren, her voice rising in a crescendo of emotion, "when a man says 'I love you' to a woman, he means, 'I choose you to be the one for me to own, possess, dominate, tame, subjugate, oppress, enslave, to be my entire staked territory over which I and only I will roam at will!' and when a woman replies, 'I love you,' she means, 'I accept all of the above!' Beware! Beware! The words that you have always thought to be music to the ear and honey on the tongue are the very poison that kills!"

A thrill of consternation ran through the audience. One woman stood up tremblingly and said, "The bastard! He has been saying 'I love you' to me every day for the last twenty years and I believed him!"

Another stood up and said with great anxiety, "All these years I could not get my live-in boyfriend to say 'I love you' to me. I would be the one to say the three words first, and he would say 'So do I'. Then last night, he did it! He said 'I love you' all on his own. You mean I have now to tell him to stop saying it?"

"Tell him," said Dora magisterially, "never to say that dirty four-letter word of enslavement again."

"What happens to our thousands of songs and poems and Valentine Day cards? Are we to empty them of their words of love?" quavered a woman who was clearly a romantic at heart.

"Put them to the bonfire," said Dora sternly. "Put an end to love. Put an end to our enslavement, sisters!"

And that was Dora's final undoing, for the women were not ready to relinguish love. Her new theory drove a cruel wedge into the sisterhood which thereafter splintered in confusion and resentment and broke away, forming their own A.D.W. or 'Against Dora Warren' groups. One of them, led by the woman who had been distressed by the prospect of never hearing her live-in boyfriend say 'I love you' again, spitefully arranged for another interview with Josie Warren who once again denounced her mother.

"'Mad, Bad and Dangerous to Know. I should know.' Says Dora Warren's Daughter," sniggered the newspapers the next day.

Dora was not daunted.

"Has Dora Warren Gone too Far? Dump Dora Warren!"

When the face with the wide eyes and gap-tooth appeared on TV, there were hisses, boos and jeers.

Dora fled into the Mexican desert once more, but this time there were no more flashing insights. Instead she slipped into deep depression and checked into a sanatorium. Then one morning, she went into the bathroom and slashed her wrists.

Click. The celestial slide-projector clicked to a stop with the last slide which was of her in the bathroom, slumped against the wall, wrists bleeding, but with a peaceful expression on her face. She was looking at herself from a height and saw the top of her head, more grey than blonde, and a rapidly spreading patch of red which was both the blood and the hibiscus print on her favourite caftan, bought during the trip to Bali, the island paradise in the Far East.

"Goodbye, I'm off!" she thought blithely, as she felt herself drifting away.

It was a wonderful sensation, this drifting, floating, gliding, sliding, whatever earth word you wanted to use for it. It was rather like the delicious sensation of small friendly waves slapping against one's body.

"Oh, this is so good," she thought, "I haven't felt this sense of peace in a long, long while. Heaven, here I come! I deserve you after the Hell they gave me on Earth!"

"Not so fast." It was a voice, a man's voice, that plucked her out of this warm amniotic bubble and put a stop to the drifting.

"Hey, you, what do you think you're doing?" cried Dora to her Guardian Angel, for that was who he was.

"I've got to take you to Transit, you cannot go to Heaven straightaway, you know," said Fordora, for that was his name.

"Transit? Oh, I understand," cried Dora cheerfully. "Like Transit at an international airport? Passports. Papers. Boarding Passes. The whole works before passing on. Heaven must be very security-sensitive!"

"Precisely," said Fordora. "Now please follow me to E-station or S-station." He paused, looked her up and down and said, "E-station, most likely, unless you can prove otherwise."

"I don't know what you are talking about; all I know is that I'm rather enjoying myself in this place which is a lot better than the old one where you get stabbed in the back by the very people you've fought for," said Dora.

"You may be speaking too soon," said Fordora.

He led her to E-station and S-Station, separated by immense, dense rolling clouds, so that their occupants, despite the abuses being hurled to and fro, could not get at each other.

"Holy Moses!" exclaimed Dora.

The E-Station had a small group of women, all looking sleek and healthy and prosperous (one Chinese woman was still wearing a fabulously expensive pair of jade earrings that she had been cremated with), but with gloomy, sullen expressions on their faces. The S-Station, on the other hand, was crowded with women in rags, half-starved, with bruised faces and bodies, but remarkably cheerful. They jeered and hissed exuberantly at the occupants of E-Station, some of whom roused themselves sufficiently from their gloom to hiss back.

Fordora explained: All women who died went to Heaven on the sheer merit of their being born women (not that he agreed with this ruling, as he quickly pointed out, but who was he, mere Guardian Angel, to be disputing rules made up there?). Not all women, however, deserved the same grade of Heaven; the greater the suffering on Earth, the higher the grade. Thus Egg-Receivers went to E-Station which was really a very low grade of Heaven only, with its own internal sub-grades, while Scorpion Receivers went to S-Station which also had its own internal levels, the highest being then occupied by a young slum woman from Calcutta who had been blinded as a child, thrown out at age five upon the street, rescued by a man who collected mutilated children to form a brigade of beggars to make money for himself, was further mutilated at age eight by having some fingers hacked off to have a competitive edge over rival beggar brigades, raped at age ten, raped and mutilated repeatedly into adulthood and finally starved to death in an airless, rat-infested hole in an alley.

She had been unanimously voted for top prize in S-Station.

"Your place is in E-Station," said Fordora. "Get ready."

"Wait a minute!" cried Dora Warren defiantly. "My place is not with those sleek, fat, prosperous and placid Egg-Receivers who never suffered. I suffered terribly. I deserve more than the minimum Heaven. I deserve to take my place with the best of the Scorpion Receivers. Oh, how my flesh had quivered to the stings of treachery!"

"They will never allow you into S-Station," said Fordora.

"Who's they?" demanded Dora.

"The Scorpion Receivers themselves," said Fordora. "They will take one look at you and hiss you all the way to E-station!"

"Now look here," said Dora belligerently. "Do you see these slashes on my wrists? Would a woman who has never suffered try to kill herself?"

"Show your slashed wrists to the Scorpion Receiver who had had both arms hacked off, or the one doused with petrol and set on fire by her husband because her dowry was insufficient, or the one called 'The Horizontal Woman' because she was precisely that, servicing thirty men a day," said Fordora savagely.

"All right, all right," said Dora pacifically. "Guardian Angels are rather given to melodrama, aren't they? But why don't you let me present myself to the Scorpion Receivers and argue my own case? I have fought so hard on behalf of women that I'm sure they'll view my case sympathetically," she concluded.

"All right, as you wish and good luck to you," said Fordora.

Dora Warren presented herself for admission to S-Station.

"You with the well-fed rump, tell me how you qualify to be one of us," snarled Rani, whose bruised and battered body had been found crushed on the railway tracks.

"Gently, gently, please, and no vulgar language," said her Guardian Angel, Forrani.

"You said you suffered. Have you any evidence of that?" jeered Amina who had been infibulated three times for her husband's bursting pleasure and had died of an infection after the third infibulation, "You want to see my evidence –"

"No need to go that far, please," said her Guardian Angel, Foramina, making a quick movement towards her to prevent the ready removal of her bead girdle, which she was always threatening upon disbelievers.

"All of you should see *my* evidence," cried the winner of the top prize who sometimes descended from the heights to show off punctured eye, hacked off limbs, rat-chewed fingers.

"For goodness' sake –," cried her Guardian Angel, Forletchmy, rushing forward to restrain her. He let out a deep sigh of weary resignation, in which he was joined by the other Guardian Angels. At their earliest opportunity, they would ask to be relieved of their present jobs and be assigned new duties.

"Wait a minute, this isn't fair," cried Dora Warren.

"Just because I haven't been bruised or burnt or battered does not mean I haven't suffered. There are hundreds, thousands of women who never received a lash or a kick in their lives but who suffered terribly. There was Charlotte Brontë for example. Her letters quivered with pain. And let me tell you this about myself, sisters. Nobody's done as much or suffered as much, fighting for the betterment of woman's lot!"

"What have you done to better woman's lot? Pray, tell us," sneered the Scorpion Receivers.

"For a start, I demythologised this whole sickening thing about Penis Envy that had kept us in thrall for decades. I developed my own Phallacy theory to counter the falsehood!"

"Did your Phallacy Theory stop the men from raping us again and again?" This from the bondmaid 'Female', raped by three generations of men and dead from a messed up abortion.

"I made women aware, for the first time, of the insidiousness of men's language. I inspired them to rise to a new sense of their dignity and identity as women!"

"Did you? Did woman's new sense of dignity and identity save her from being sold into prostitution by her own parents?" from the little Thai girl, sold as a 'Virgin Prostitute' in a Bangkok hotel to cater to aging libidos.

"Oh, but listen! I forced men to stop using only female

names for hurricanes, typhoons and other horrid natural disasters and to use male names too. That compelled them to make an amazing paradigm shift, I can tell you!"

"Did your paradigm shift stop fathers from cursing at newborn baby girls so that their frightened mothers would no longer have to kill them at birth or throw them into dustbins?" cried a small, unnamed baby girl still with the strangling rag round her neck, while her Guardian Angel, Fornoname, said soothingly, "There, there, it's all right. No need to get so upset!"

"Oh, please listen –" begged Dora, but there arose such a cacophony of hisses, shrieks, yells and curses that she retreated hastily and went running, in tears, to her Guardian Angel.

"I told you," he said wearily, "but you wouldn't listen."

"I suppose I'll have to be contented with E-Station. Dammit! I had hoped that having gone through so much on Earth, I would deserve more in Heaven!"

"Hey, look who's here!" said Fordora and he turned, with pleasure, to greet a fellow Guardian Angel whom he had not seen for a long time.

"Hello, Forcharlotte!" cried Fordora heartily. "And what brings you here?'

"Your charge," said Forcharlotte, "My charge wants to speak to her. See here she comes!" A small prim-looking woman with a severe face and equally severe hairstyle appeared.

"Charlotte Brontë!" gasped Dora Warren. "Fancy meeting you here. I didn't see you in E or S-Station."

"I'm in E," said the lady matter-of-factly, "Listen, I

was observing the proceedings just now with great interest and seeing from the start that you stood no chance. Women like ourselves have never made it to S, because, compared to them, we have never known what real suffering is. I only discovered this here. We are the Egg-Receivers and they the Scorpion Receivers. There's just no comparison. Take my advice. Be content with E," and the lady turned to go and slowly disappeared, followed by her Guardian Angel, who clearly adored her.

"What do you think I should do now?" Dora Warren asked her Guardian Angel dispiritedly.

"There are special cases like yours in which we Guardian Angels are authorised to use our judgement," said Fordora. "And this is what I will do. I am giving you a choice: you either move on to E-Station or return to Earth and see whether you can accumulate the necessary merit to deserve S. Of course I don't promise you will get S the next time, but I'm just offering you a choice."

Into Dora Warren's mind had suddenly flashed a scene which she thought she had dismissed long ago. She saw again the woman on the Allahabad railway platform, crawling out of her rags with her baby, past the money on the ground, in an attempt to touch her with her stump of an arm. She saw herself, not fleeing in terror this time, but crawling to meet this woman, crawling past her theories, past her demythologising and paradigms and syndromes, to meet and touch.

"I think I have made my choice," she said, "Thank you, Fordora."

* * *

"Mother, are you all right?" said Josie gently, bending over her as she lay on the hospital bed. She looked around and then down at her bandaged wrists. She felt so tired.

"Mother, you gave us such a fright," continued Josie, "but you're okay now, so try to get some sleep, Mother darling." She was with a boyfriend whom she was going to marry soon, and in her new happiness, was sorry she ever said those nasty things about her mother at the interviews.

Dora continued looking around wearily, then started up, remembering something, and a new look of purpose came into her eyes and brightened them. Seeing a nurse come in, she asked, "Nurse, how soon before I can get up and go on a trip?"

"Heavens, Mrs Warren, you shouldn't be thinking of trips just yet!" laughed the nurse good-naturedly.

"Josie, could you book me a flight to India, to Allahabad? Soon. Now."

"Yes, yes, of course, Mother," said Josie and she and her boyfriend and the nurse exchanged glances that said, "Dora Warren is far, far from well. She will have to be under observation for a long time."

"Of course, Mother," repeated Josie, settling her back gently on her pillows, "but first you must have a good rest."

"Thanks," said Dora, and was soon asleep.

About the author

"I would like to describe myself as a true chronicler of the human condition. True and caring."

—Catherine Lim

Catherine Lim is a full-time writer and has published collections of short stories, a novel and a book of poems. Her books have been used as literature texts at home and abroad, and have been translated into Chinese, Japanese and Tagalog.

Catherine, who holds a PhD in applied linguistics, lives in Singapore and has two grown-up children.

By the same publisher

The Serpent's Tooth **(1982)**
by Catherine Lim
Within each family lie the proverbial skeletons better left untouched, lest the truths uncovered become too horrifying. *The Serpent's Tooth* is fraught with dashed hopes and wasted efforts, where characters grope around desperately in the murky depths of self-delusion. Where hands reach beyond the grave, and resurface to haunt.

Under bestselling author Catherine Lim's deft treatment of Asian superstition, myths and legends, this absorbing book tells of the past that collides with the present as dreams and nightmares turn into alarming reality.

They Do Return **(1983)**
by Catherine Lim
Lurking at the fringes of reality is another dimension that many scoff at but few really dare to dismiss. The supernatural – simultaneously held with dread and an awed fascination. From the wellspring of her imaginative

powers Catherine Lim produces these tales of the supernatural against an Asian setting.

Unlike the bloodthirsty, sensational stories favoured at gatherings and holiday chalets, these stories are quietly told, emphasizing commonplace realities underlying even the most shocking events. There are those relationships which death cannot sever, or those personalities so strong that they invade the land of the living after death. Some of the stories have no direct bearing on the supernatural, but instead reflect their significance in the Asian context.

***O Singapore! Stories in Celebration* (1989)**
by Catherine Lim

From the playfully satirical pen of Catherine Lim comes the wild, weird and wacky world of *O Singapore!* This is modern day Singapore where the campaigns and the directives of the unremittingly competent leadership come face to face with the undeniably human fads, foibles and follies of the Singaporean people. A world where public policy and private life collide. Using some of the traits which Singaporeans have good naturedly identified themselves with – materialism, money-mindedness, 'Kiasuism' (calculating, self-protecting behaviour) and 'Humsubism' (a brand of lecherousness said to be peculiar to Chinese males) as focal points, Catherine Lim takes us through the dizzying whirl of these merry collisions with consummate wit and inventiveness.